Yes, Duke Jenkins thought, marrying Dani Adams would work out for everyone.

Dani would have a ready-made family. His sons would have a mother's love again. And him? He'd already admitted that he was attracted to her. And the prospect of having her in his life wasn't nearly as distasteful as he'd expected, given his determination not to remarry.

Duke always trusted his instincts. He also made decisions in a rush and stuck by them.

He wondered how he'd present his scheme to Dani. She struck him as a woman who might not be nearly as pragmatic as he was, even under her own currently vulnerable circumstances. She might prefer at least the pretense of romance.

When Dani turned toward him, he lifted his beer mug in a silent toast. Anticipation sizzled through his veins like fine champagne. Yes, indeed, life in Los Pinos promised to get downright fascinating.

Dear Reader,

In celebration of Valentine's Day, we have a Special Edition lineup filled with love and romance!

Cupid reignites passion between two former lovebirds in this month's THAT'S MY BABY! title. *Valentine Baby* by Gina Wilkins is about a fallen firefighter who returns home on Valentine's Day to find a baby—and his former sweetheart offering a shocking marriage proposal!

Since so many of you adored Silhouette's MONTANA MAVERICKS series, we have a special treat in store for you over the next few months in Special Edition. Jackie Merritt launches the MONTANA MAVERICKS: RETURN TO WHITEHORN series with a memorable story about a lovelorn cowboy and the woman who makes his life complete, in *Letter to a Lonesome Cowboy.* And coming up are three more books in the series as well as a delightful collection of short stories and an enthralling Harlequin Historical title.

These next three books showcase how children can bond people together in the most miraculous ways. In *Wildcatter's Kid,* by Penny Richards, a young lad reunites his parents. This is the final installment of the SWITCHED AT BIRTH miniseries. Next, *Natural Born Trouble,* by veteran author Sherryl Woods—the second book in her AND BABY MAKES THREE: THE NEXT GENERATION miniseries—is an uplifting story about a reserved heroine who falls for the charms of rambunctious twin boys...and their sexy father! And a sweet seven-year-old inspires a former rebel to reclaim his family, in *Daddy's Home,* by Pat Warren.

Finally, Celeste Hamilton unfolds an endearing tale about two childhood pals who make all their romantic dreams come true, in *Honeymoon Ranch.*

I hope you enjoy this book and each and every title to come!

Sincerely,

Tara Gavin,
Senior Editor and Editorial Coordinator

Please address questions and book requests to:
Silhouette Reader Service
U.S.: 3010 Walden Ave., P.O. Box 1325, Buffalo, NY 14269
Canadian: P.O. Box 609, Fort Erie, Ont. L2A 5X3

SHERRYL WOODS

NATURAL BORN TROUBLE

SPECIAL EDITION®

Published by Silhouette Books
America's Publisher of Contemporary Romance

SILHOUETTE BOOKS

ISBN 0-373-24156-9

NATURAL BORN TROUBLE

Printed in U.S.A.

Books by Sherryl Woods

Silhouette Special Edition

Safe Harbor #425
Never Let Go #446
Edge of Forever #484
In Too Deep #522
Miss Liz's Passion #573
Tea and Destiny #595
My Dearest Cal #669
Joshua and the Cowgirl #713
*Love #769
*Honor #775
*Cherish #781
*Kate's Vow #823
*A Daring Vow #855
*A Vow To Love #885
The Parson's Waiting #907
One Step Away #927
Riley's Sleeping Beauty #961
†*Finally a Bride* #987
‡*A Christmas Blessing* #1001
‡*Natural Born Daddy* #1007
‡*The Cowboy and His Baby* #1009
‡*The Rancher and His Unexpected
  Daughter* #1016
**A Ranch for Sara #1083
***Ashley's Rebel* #1087
***Danielle's Daddy Factor* #1094
††*The Littlest Angel* #1142
††*Natural Born Trouble* #1156

Silhouette Desire

Not at Eight, Darling #309
Yesterday's Love #329
Come Fly with Me #345
A Gift of Love #375
Can't Say No #431
Heartland #472
One Touch of Moondust #521
Next Time...Forever #601
Fever Pitch #620
Dream Mender #708

Silhouette Books

Silhouette Summer Sizzlers 1990
"A Bridge to Dreams"

*Vows
†Always a Bridesmaid!
‡And Baby Makes Three
**The Bridal Path
††And Baby Makes Three:
The Next Generation

SHERRYL WOODS

lives by the ocean, which, she says, provides daily inspiration for the romance in her soul. She further explains that her years as a television critic taught her about steamy plots and humor; her years as a travel editor took her to exotic locations; and her years as a crummy weekend tennis player taught her to stick with what she enjoyed most—writing. "What better way is there," Sherryl asks, "to combine all that experience than by creating romantic stories?" Sherryl loves to hear from her readers. You may write to her at P.O. Box 490326, Key Biscayne, FL 33149. A self-addressed, stamped envelope is appreciated for a reply.

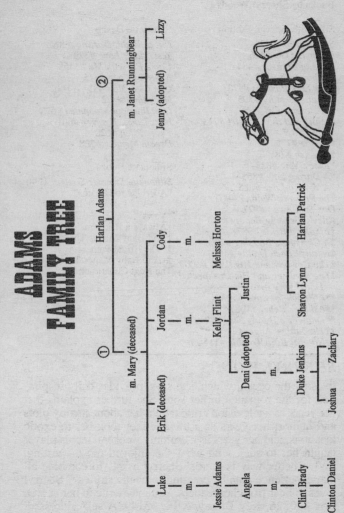

ADAMS FAMILY TREE

Harlan Adams

① m. Mary (deceased)

② m. Janet Runningbear

Jenny (adopted) — Lizzy

Luke — m. Jessie Adams

Erik (deceased)

Jordan — m. Kelly Flint

Cody — m. Melissa Horton

Angela — m. Clint Brady

Clinton Daniel

Dani (adopted) — m. Duke Jenkins

Justin

Joshua — Zachary

Sharon Lynn — Harlan Patrick

Chapter One

The day had already been too long and it wasn't even noon.

Dani Adams sank down into the chair behind her desk and vowed to catch a quick nap before her afternoon appointments. She'd been up since three a.m. with an emergency, a dog that had been struck by a drunk driver on a flat stretch of Texas highway just outside of town.

The sheriff's urgent call, when he was already en route, had awakened her. Minutes later, he had brought the bruised and bloodied animal in, and she'd worked for hours trying to save it. The poor old thing was hanging on by a thread.

She probably should have put him to sleep, but every time she thought of his owner, eighty-year-old Betty Lou Parks, she balked. Betty Lou adored that dog. He was her constant companion, riding beside her in the rusty old car Betty Lou drove into town once a week to pick up groceries. Dani had heard the anxiety and choked-back tears in Betty Lou's quavery voice when she'd called to check on her beloved pet and that had been that. Dani had promised to do everything she could to save the old woman's precious Honeybunch.

Honeybunch, she thought, smiling. The poor dog was probably embarrassed every time his master called to him in public. Mostly proud German shepherd, he had just enough mixed blood in him to give him a slightly whimsical look. Dani knew better than to be fooled by his appearance, though. He was fiercely protective of Betty Lou, which was probably why her children hadn't insisted long ago that she move into town from the isolated house where she still planted a garden every single spring.

Dani suspected most of her fee would come from that garden. Tomatoes, potatoes, beans, squash, herbs. Betty Lou raised them all, more than enough to last her through winter and to barter for some of her other needs. She was as independent now as she had been fifty years ago when her husband had died and left her alone with three small children to care for. Dani admired her resilience. She could use a little of it now just to get her through the rest of the day.

Sighing when her mind kept whirling and sleep eluded her, she picked up the batch of mail her assistant had left on her desk and out of habit sorted it into neatly organized stacks. Bills went into one pile, junk mail into another, professional newsletters and magazines into a third. When she came to a cheap business-sized envelope addressed in childish printing, her heart skidded to a halt. Automatic and too-familiar tears stung her eyes.

She already knew what she would find inside, a crayon-bright picture and a precisely lettered note. She had a whole drawer full of them, all from Rob Hilliard's two girls, children who had almost been hers.

Even after two years, every time one of these envelopes came it tore her apart inside all over again. Walking away from Robin and Amy when things hadn't worked out with their father had been the hardest thing Dani had ever had to do. For a time the envelopes had stacked up, unopened, because to see these expressions of love and know that she would never be a parent to the children who created them broke her heart. Phone calls left her shattered for hours, sometimes days.

Had she and Rob been married, had she been a real mother to the girls, at least there would have been the kind of custody arrangements that came with divorce. The girls would be with her part—if not all—of the time.

As it was, she had no rights, no legal standing whatsoever in their lives, just the powerful bond of a love that had deepened over the four years she had been with their father. Four years, during which expectations of permanence had been raised. An engagement that had sealed that expectation. Wedding plans had consumed Dani's thoughts and enchanted the girls.

And then it had all come tumbling down. Rob had met someone else and broken the engagement just weeks before the scheduled wedding date. Dani had been crushed. The girls, understanding none of what was going on, had been devastated when Dani had moved out of the house and left town.

Now distance and the attitude of Rob's young and insecure girlfriend precluded even the most casual of visits. Tiffany thought the girls would adjust more readily if the break were clean. Tiffany thought... Tiffany thought... Dani hadn't seen much evidence that Tiffany even had a brain.

As soon as the sarcastic criticism surfaced, Dani chided herself for being uncharitable. It was hardly Tiffany's fault that Rob had no spine to speak of.

At any rate, contact had been limited to whatever calls and drawings the seven-year-old and five-year-old girls could manage. They'd been astonishingly ingenious about it, too.

Now, though, they were slowly adapting to the change. The vows to hate Tiffany forever and ever were less frequent. So were the calls and notes to Dani. The spaces in between almost gave her time to heal, but it took only an envelope like this one to rip the wound open all over again and leave her feeling raw and vulnerable. How did adoptive mothers stand it when courts ripped their children from their arms to return them to the natural parents? How did they survive the loss? she wondered. How did they make the love stop? Or fill the empty space inside their heart?

For a moment she debated leaving the envelope

unopened, but there seemed little point to it. Sooner or later she would open it anyway. Like removing a bandage with a sudden yank, this would be quicker, if no less painful.

The sheet of paper inside was a piece of Rob's expensive, embossed business stationery, she noted with amusement. He would probably have a cow if he knew they'd gotten into it and used it for coloring.

She studied the page, her eyes misty. Amy had clearly done the drawing. It was as vibrantly colorful as the little girl herself. A shaky American flag predominated, dwarfing two stick-figure children—Robin and Amy, according to the names neatly printed under them by the older Robin. Each child was holding what Dani assumed were meant to be sparklers.

"Happy Fourth of July" was printed across the top in red and blue letters. "We Miss You" had been added in bright pink and purple at the bottom. "Love, Robin" was as precise as a seven-year-old hand could make it. Amy's signature was twice the size of her sister's and bore little evidence of any understanding of capital and small letters.

"Oh, babies," Dani murmured. "I miss you, too." She stared at the picture for as long as she could bear it, then tucked it into the drawer with all the others. She would answer the note tonight, though she had no idea if the petty Tiffany allowed the children to see the occasional cards and letters Dani sent to them so they would know that she still thought of them and loved them, that she hadn't deliberately abandoned them.

The knock on her office door had her hurriedly wiping away telltale traces of tears.

"Yes, Maggie, what is it?"

Her nineteen-year-old temporary assistant poked her head in. She was clearly fighting a smile. "I'm really sorry to interrupt you. I know you need a break after the night you had, but we have an emergency up front."

"It's not Honeybunch, is it?" she asked, already pulling her white coat on over her slacks and short-sleeved blouse.

"No, no, it's nothing like that," Maggie soothed in a calming tone that proved what a good vet she, too, would make one day. "I think you'd better come and see for yourself."

Dani followed her assistant down the corridor to the reception area. Even before they got there, she could hear two voices. They were arguing. They were also very young.

"Told you not to take him out of the bowl," one was saying.

"I didn't," the other replied. "Not for long anyway."

Dani glanced at Maggie. The teen's lips were twitching with amusement again.

"I can't go back out there," Maggie said, drawing to a halt outside one of the treatment rooms. "I know I'll laugh and obviously this is a very serious crisis to them."

"Let me guess," Dani said. "We're not talking a puppy or a kitten here, are we?"

"Afraid not."

"A goldfish?" Dani guessed.

"You got it."

"Dead?"

"Oh, yes."

Dani closed her eyes and sighed. "You could have handled this, you know."

"Not me. I haven't even finished pre-vet school," Maggie said. "Besides, they wanted a real veterinarian. Said they could pay, too. Fifty cents."

"Terrific. Just terrific."

Plastering a smile on her face, she stepped into the reception area and confronted two boys, no more than eight, identical twins from the look of them. Both had spiky blond hair and freckles and the same front tooth missing. If she hadn't made up her mind never to let another child get to her, these two would have stolen her heart on the spot. As it was, she cloaked herself in a brisk, professional demeanor.

"I'm Dr. Dani Adams," she told them. "What seems to be the problem?"

"You're a girl," one of them said, eyes wide.

"Yeah, we wanted a real doctor," the other stated firmly. "Not a nurse."

Chauvinist little devils, she concluded, trying very hard not to bristle.

"I am a doctor. You can see my license, if you like. It's hanging over my desk."

The two boys looked at each other, seemed to reach a silent, joint conclusion, then nodded.

"I guess it's okay," one said with unflattering reluctance. "Show her, Zachary."

A smudged little hand emerged from a pocket. Zachary opened his fist to display a sizable, but very dead goldfish.

"We think he might be a goner," Zachary said, tears obviously threatening. "Can you save him?"

Dani hunkered down in front of them and took the patient. "I won't lie to you. It's serious, all right. Let me take him in the back and see if there's anything I can do."

The second twin regarded her suspiciously. "Can we come?"

"I think you'd better wait out here," she said. "I promise I won't be long."

Fortunately, she had learned long ago working for the last town vet to expect anything. She kept a drawer filled with suitable pet "coffins." In the back she placed the dead goldfish atop some cotton in an old jewelry box, waited a suitable length of time, then started for the front, struggling to keep her expression serious. Maggie was having no such luck, though she was trying to stifle her chuckles.

"Hush," Dani whispered as she passed.

Back out front she found the two boys once again trying to place blame. Worried gazes shot up when she returned. At the sight of the box, lower lips trembled and tears clearly threatened.

"He's a goner, isn't he?" Zachary asked pitifully.

"I'm sorry," she said quietly, handing the box to him. He took it gingerly, clearly more intimidated now that he knew the fish was indeed dead. "It was too late. There was nothing I could do. Goldfish really don't do very well outside their bowls."

The indignant owner of the goldfish poked his brother. "Told you, dimwit."

"Listen, Joshua Michael Jenkins, you don't know everything," Zachary said, punching his brother back and allowing the boxed-up goldfish to topple to the floor in the process.

Dani stepped between them and quieted them with a hand on each boy's shoulder. "Hey, you two, don't start taking this out on each other. It was an accident, I'm sure."

"It wasn't no accident," Joshua said, scowling. "He was jealous 'cause my goldfish lived and his didn't, so he killed it on purpose."

"Did not," Zachary said, trying to slip around Dani to throw a punch.

In his haste, he barely missed the box he'd dropped. Dani retrieved it. No telling what would happen if he squished his brother's fish on top of having killed it.

Dani hunkered down again and circled an arm around both waists, forcing them to remain where they were. "Were these your only pets?"

"Yeah," Joshua said. "Dad said until we could learn to be responsible and take care of a couple of goldfish, he wasn't getting us no puppy."

Dani winced at the appalling grammar, but figured someone better qualified than she was should be correcting that. "He's right, you know. If you own animals, it's very important that you take good care of them. It is a responsibility."

"We'll probably never get a dog now," Joshua grumbled. "And it's all your fault, dimwit. I coulda had one. It wasn't my goldfish that died, not until you killed it.''

"Maybe there's a way you could change your father's mind," Dani said.

They eyed her skeptically.

"I don't know," Zachary said. "Dad's pretty strict. Once he lays down the law, he won't budge for nothing."

"How?" Joshua asked, clearly more willing to consider any option that would get him the puppy he wanted.

"Well, you see, I have a lot of kittens around here. People bring their cats by all the time, and I try to find good homes for them and their babies."

Joshua appeared mildly intrigued. "Kittens, huh? What does that have to do with us?"

"I was thinking that perhaps your dad might let you bring one home on a trial basis until I could find a real home for it. It would be temporary, of course. I know it's not a substitute for the puppy you want, but it would help me out and you two could prove to your dad that you are responsible enough for a puppy. What do you think?"

"Could we see the kittens?" Zachary asked.

"Sure."

Dani led the way through the clinic to the entry into her own living quarters. Francie III, a descendant of her own first cat, lounged under the kitchen table, where she had the benefit of the cool linoleum and a slanted beam of sunlight.

"Is that the one?" Joshua asked, eyes wide. "She's really, really big."

"She's expecting babies," Dani explained.

At the sound of her voice, more cats scrambled through the doorway, skidding on the waxed floor, then meowing plaintively for food as they wound themselves around her ankles. The cats gave wide berth to the two boys. Maybe on some subliminal pet network they'd heard about the goldfish.

Three kittens, not quite as fast as the adults, nor as discriminating, picked their way daintily toward two pairs of fascinating new sneaker-clad feet and sniffed.

The boys peered down at the scrambling, tumbling heap of kittens, two gray-and-white, one orange with white paws.

"I like the orange one," Zachary said.

"Me, too," Joshua said. "He looks like a tiger."

"It's a girl," Dani said.

"Does she have a name?"

"Not yet, but I'll bet she'd really like one. You two could name her, if you're interested."

"Mittens," Zachary said at once.

"That's a dumb name," Joshua protested.

"Is not. Her paws are white, aren't they?" Zachary bent down to pick up the kitten, but Joshua promptly nudged him aside.

"Don't even think about touching her," he said. "You'll probably squish her or something."

"Will not."

"Will, too."

"Hey," Dani protested. "If you two can't get along and work together to take care of her, then I can't suggest to your dad that he allow you to watch out for her for me."

"You're going to talk to our dad?" Zachary asked, wide-eyed.

"Of course. I can't send the kitten home with you without his permission. If you'd like me to, I'll call him right now."

"At work?" Joshua asked, then shook his head. "I don't think that's such a good idea. He's not in a very good mood when he's at work."

"Besides I don't think he'd like it very much if he knew Paolina brought us into town," Zachary added.

"Paolina?"

"She's our new housekeeper," Joshua explained.

"Yeah, and she's stayed a whole two weeks, longer than any of the others."

"I see." Dani hid a smile at the telling remarks. "You let me worry about your dad. I think he'll understand that this was a crisis. Do you know the number?" She picked up a nearby portable phone.

"Sure," Zachary said and recited it.

The familiar number had her pausing. "Your dad's in the oil business?"

"How'd you know that?" Joshua asked.

"I know someone who works there," she said carefully, not mentioning that the someone was her stepfather, nor that he owned the company. "What's your dad's name?"

"Duke Jenkins."

Ah, Dani thought, so these boys belonged to the mysterious Duke Jenkins, whose reputation in the field had been legendary. She'd overheard Jordan talking about how badly he hated the thought of losing him on exploration, but what an asset he would be anywhere in the company.

She'd also heard that the man was chafing at being chained to a desk. She suspected these two had something to do with his decision to take a safer assignment. Or perhaps his wife had demanded it. Then, again, hadn't she heard he was a widower? Or was he divorced? Either would explain why he and not their mother was making the decisions about their pets and why this new housekeeper was so important.

She hit speed dial for the company headquarters a few blocks away. Originally the company had been in Houston, but her mother had persuaded Jordan to relocate years ago. When the operator answered, Dani greeted her, then asked for Duke Jenkins.

"Don't tell me you've staked him out already," the young woman said with an audible sigh of regret.

"Actually, I'm calling on a business matter," Dani reassured her.

"Well, you're out of luck, hon. He's in with Jordan and last time I checked the rafters were about to blow straight off the building. I wouldn't buzz in there for the president of the U.S.A."

Donna Kelso was not easily intimidated, nor was Jordan the kind of man who tolerated much insubordination. Dani could only imagine just how explosive the meeting going on in her stepfather's office was. If Duke Jenkins was foolish enough to take Jordan on, he was either a very brave man or he operated on pure arrogance. If Jordan hadn't fired him in the first five minutes, then Duke Jenkins was a very valuable company asset. Dani knew better than to get caught in the middle.

"Never mind," she said hurriedly. "I'll catch up with him later. Thanks, Donna."

"You bet. You want me to leave him a message, say in a day or two when things cool down?"

"No, thanks."

She hung up and turned to see two very disappointed faces.

"I guess we don't get a kitten, huh?" Zachary asked.

"Not right away," she said. "But I will talk to your dad. I promise."

"When?" Joshua asked. "Tonight? He's always home by suppertime. You could come over. That would be best. Dad would never yell at a lady in person. He says it's not proper to hit girls and yell at them and stuff."

Dani wasn't at all sure she wanted to meet the formidable Duke Jenkins on his home turf, especially when his mood was likely to be surly. Still, she really did have to find a home for the kittens. She had a hunch a face-to-face chat with Mr. Jenkins was the only way these boys were going to get permission to bring one home. Besides, it might be interesting to see what sort of scars Duke Jenkins bore from his battle with Jordan. She'd known few men who dared to stand up to him and lived to tell about it, other than her uncles and grandfather, of course.

"I'll stop by as soon as I close up for the day," she agreed.

"Will you bring the kitten with you?" Joshua asked hopefully.

She shook her head. "That might be a tactical mistake, boys. I'd better talk to your dad first."

"He would probably like Mittens a lot if he saw her," Zachary argued.

"Trust me," Dani said, thinking that Zachary's tactical approach was very reminiscent of one she had used quite often at his age. Now she reacted with an adult's sense of caution. "We should get his permission first."

Let the man at least think he was in charge. It was a motto that made sense to her. It didn't mean he had to actually be in charge, as long as he thought he was. Being around a whole clan of master manipulators, most of them hardheaded males, had given her an edge on understanding the masculine thought process. She doubted Duke Jenkins veered too far from the same mold. In fact, Donna's report had just pretty much confirmed it.

"Dr. Adams?" Joshua asked, sounding suspiciously meek.

"Yes?" She noticed his gaze was pinned to the kittens again.

Blue eyes lifted and regarded her hopefully. "As long as you're going to talk to Dad anyway, do you think maybe you could see if we could keep all three kittens?" Joshua asked. "One for me and one for Zack and one for Dad."

"I don't know," she said. "Maybe we should start with just one. Besides, your dad might not want a kitten of his own."

"I'll bet he would," Zachary said. "He's kinda lonely now that Mom's gone."

Definitely another budding manipulator, she thought, fighting the salty sting of tears at the hitch in his voice. Probably a trait he'd picked up at his father's knee. That reference to his mom was definitely calculated to stir sympathy.

No problem, though. She was an Adams, by name and upbringing, if not by birth. When it came to manipulation, she had learned from the best authorities in the whole state of Texas, if not the entire world. Resisting Duke Jenkins and his sons would be a snap.

Then she recalled Donna's awestruck reaction at the mention of Duke's name. Maybe now would be a good time to start praying that she wasn't unwittingly about to start flirting with disaster.

Chapter Two

Duke Jenkins was mad enough to bend a steel beam in two, preferably around Jordan Adams's neck. The man was stubborn, arrogant and, without question, the best oil man in the state of Texas. Maybe in the world. Duke figured he was no slouch himself, which suggested that maybe once, just once, Jordan ought to listen to him.

They were going to be wasting time and money drilling that new field. Every instinct he possessed told him that. He didn't give two hoots about the ream of geological surveys piled up on his desk. If he'd been able to get out there and look things over first-hand, run the dirt through his fingers, get a deep whiff of the scent of it, he would have been able to put some real strength into his arguments.

As it was, he was going with his gut, instinct honed

by years of wildcatting. Jordan preferred cold, hard facts. Scientific facts, which in this instance Duke suspected had been doctored to someone else's benefit.

If he'd had somebody to look after the boys, Duke would have given Jordan all the facts he wanted. He would have been on a plane in a heartbeat, doing what he did best: finding oil and bringing it in, making them all richer.

Not that he cared all that much about the money. Most of his life he hadn't had a lot, hadn't needed much. Now he just wanted to insure that his sons would have a good future, a college education if they wanted it, though getting them through elementary school was proving to be challenge enough.

At any rate, he would trade the potential profits for the pure adrenaline rush of bringing in a new gusher any day.

Instead, he was surrounded by paperwork, mounds of it, most of which didn't matter a tinker's damn in the overall scheme of things as near as he could tell.

Oh, how he hated pushing papers around on a desk, he thought, staring irritably at the mostly untouched piles of it still awaiting some action or another. Well, today he'd had enough of it, he concluded, grabbing his jacket and heading for the door. If he hung around another few minutes, he might storm straight back into Jordan's office and quit, something he didn't have the right to do with two kids depending on him. The twins were the reason he'd made the move to Los Pinos in the first place. He had to give this major life-style overhaul a chance to work for their sakes.

Twenty minutes later, he had the top on the classic

convertible down, the car radio was blaring a George Strait tune and he was curving down the winding driveway to the white, ranch-style house he'd bought on the outskirts of Los Pinos. There was a little dip in the land, then a rise. His house was nestled in that suggestion of a valley, surrounded by the pines for which the town had been named. A trickle of water that passed for a creek was the north boundary of the property. It looked like a picture-book image of what a home ought to be. He'd bought it at first sight because of that. It had triggered some sort of subliminal yearning within him.

Not that he had much experience with real homes. He'd bounced from foster home to foster home as a kid, a born troublemaker, according to those in the system who'd had to deal with his belligerence.

Used to being on the move, he'd seen no need to settle down once he'd grown up. Oil had been a way to stay on the go and pile up a decent bankroll.

Given his total lack of experience with lasting relationships, he probably never should have married, but Caroline had convinced him that they could make it work. When she'd been whispering in his ear late at night, when her magical hands had been busy moving over him, he believed almost anything that came out of her mouth.

Unfortunately, she hadn't counted on his refusal to quit wandering wherever the excitement took him. At first, she had gone with him, but once the boys had come along, she'd insisted on staying in one place. A few years of that and she'd gotten lonely and frustrated. When he was home, there had been more fights than loving.

A few months back, she had walked out, claiming that she'd had the twins to raise all alone for most of the past eight years, now he could see for himself how much fun it was. He could call her when he'd put in equal time and maybe they would work out a new arrangement.

Duke wasn't counting on it. He figured the divorce papers he'd received in the mail almost immediately pretty much countered any hopes he might have been harboring that things would eventually return to normal.

Even so, for a solid month he'd tried to pretend that nothing had changed. He'd convinced himself that he could go right on working crazy hours, taking off at the drop of a hat. Reality had slammed in when the fourth housekeeper in as many weeks quit in a huff.

Just in case the message wasn't plain enough, Zachary broke his arm and Joshua brought home a report card that suggested he hadn't cracked a book since his mother left. Even Duke had been bright enough to figure out that it was time to grow up and take responsibility for his sons, that parenting wasn't something a man could do in his spare time.

Not that he hadn't loved them all along. He had. He adored them. In fact, he was in awe of them. They were bright and mischievous and loving. He just didn't know a doggone thing about day-in, day-out caregiving. But he could learn, by God. There were books on the subject. He supposed there were even shrinks who specialized in that kind of stuff, not that he would ever be caught dead talking to one.

He did buy the books, though. A dozen of them the first week. When he caught the boys reading them, he figured he was never going to get an edge unless he worked at parenting full-time. With a sinking sensation in the pit of his stomach, he had hitched a ride in the corporate jet and had a long talk with Jordan Adams. Jordan came from a long line of men who understood about family. He'd offered Duke a vice presidency in Los Pinos on the spot. With it came the promise of stability.

Two weeks later, Duke had a new job and a new home. Moving in a hurry was something at which he excelled. It remained to be seen if he could get the rest of it right.

As he stepped out of the car in front of that appealing new home, the boys came barreling out the front door. It was a scene straight out of an old "Father Knows Best" episode and for a moment he allowed a feeling of immense satisfaction to steal over him. Not that it would last. His kids were irreverent little imps who would never be confused with anybody's angelic offspring for long.

"Don't let the screen door slam," Duke hollered just as it rocked on its hinges. He winced at the sound. He figured that door, the hinges and the frame would last a month, tops. Fortunately for all of them, he was reasonably handy with tools.

"Sorry, Dad," Joshua said unconvincingly.

"Yeah, sorry," Zack echoed.

Already stripped of his jacket and tie himself, he

noted that they were looking a little more like normal kids again, with dirt streaking their faces and rips in their T-shirts. There had been one awful period when they'd been so neat and tidy he hadn't recognized them, just as he often didn't recognize himself in the business suits he was wearing these days. The boys' transition had been the fault of the second house-keeper. Or was it the third? Anyway, she'd had a very rigid outlook. She was the only one Duke had actually had to fire. She'd seemed to enjoy the challenge of turning his sons into proper young men a little too much.

"Hey, Dad, guess what?" Zachary said.

"Hush," his brother hissed.

"What?" Duke asked, suspicion aroused by the exchange.

Zack scowled at his brother. "We gotta tell him. She's coming right now."

"Who's coming now?" Duke asked. He glanced up the driveway and saw that, indeed, a four-wheel-drive vehicle of some kind was kicking up dust. "Okay, guys, what's up? What kind of trouble are you in?"

"We're not in any trouble," Joshua claimed. "Honest, Dad."

The last time Duke had heard that he discovered that they had broken a neighbor's window—his very large, floor-to-ceiling window. It had cost an arm and a leg to repair it. He would be taking the money out of their allowances until they reached puberty.

Since the truth seemed to be in short supply coming

from these two, he decided to wait to see what the new arrival would have to say.

He studied the car as it came closer. Expensive and trendy once, it was little more than serviceable now. There was a layer of dried dirt, topped by dust over most of it, muting a dark green paint into something closer to muddy moss. For a man who took his cars seriously, this one was enough to make him shudder. He had an automatic hankering to rush for a hose and a can of his best wax.

The woman who emerged, however, had him shuddering for another, far more positive reason entirely. She was a beauty. Long legs and skinny behind were molded by denim. The suggestion of very interesting curves lurked beneath a short-sleeved silk blouse that had been tied at a waist he could span with his hands. Blond hair, scooped into some sort of ponytail, escaped in curling tendrils to frame a face that was lovely even without makeup. He'd seen that face somewhere before, but for the life of him he couldn't remember where. As for the rest of her, he wouldn't have forgotten that in a dozen lifetimes, so apparently they'd never actually met.

A model, maybe? She was tall and thin enough. An actress? With that golden complexion and blue-gray eyes, she had a face the camera would love. Still, it didn't quite fit. Besides, Los Pinos, Texas, wasn't exactly crawling with the rich and famous. The town wasn't quaint enough to draw tourists. Nor was it home to any celebrities he'd ever heard of.

While his mind sorted through alternate possibilities, she crossed to where they were standing in three

brisk strides. He wondered if she realized that the
sway of her hips robbed her movements of the professional demeanor she was clearly after. She nodded
at the boys, who were suddenly, inexplicably very
quiet, then held out her hand.

"Hi, I'm Dr. Danielle Adams. Everyone calls me
Dani."

Her voice was so low, so blasted seductive that her
title and name barely registered. Duke took her hand
in his and felt a jolt of pure electricity charge through
him. He didn't feel much inclined to let her go, but
she subtly wrestled her hand away from him. The
reaction made him smile. So, he thought with satisfaction, she'd felt it, too. Hadn't liked it half as much
as he had, though.

"Duke Jenkins," he said. "What can I do for
you?"

"I'm the vet in Los Pinos," she said.

His gaze narrowed. Adams? A veterinarian? The
pieces suddenly clicked into place and a sinking sensation settled in his stomach.

"You're Jordan's daughter," he guessed, remembering where he'd seen that face. It was very promi-
nently displayed on his boss's desk, right alongside a
much less interesting framed photo of his son and a
family portrait taken some years back, when this
woman had still been in pigtails.

"Yes," she said. Then, as if she were anxious to
get past the subject of family ties, she rushed on with
some convoluted tale of dead goldfish and kittens.

"I have all three of them in the car, if you'd like
to take a look. I think the boys could really learn a

lot taking responsibility for them, don't you?'' she concluded, her eyes locked hopefully on his. He noticed they were more blue than gray just now as if some inner fire had sparked the sapphire in them.

Duke struggled to sort out the tale. When he had, he stared at her incredulously. ''They killed two goldfish in less than a week, and you want me to let them care for three kittens? Doesn't that strike you as a bit risky?''

She gave him a winning smile that almost caused his heart to slam to a stop. Logic flew out the window. He wanted desperately to do as she asked, anything she asked.

''Really, it's not the same thing at all,'' she assured him. ''Cats, even kittens, are reasonably independent and self-sufficient. And this would be temporary. I'm in a bit of a bind, you see. I have to find homes for these three, plus two more that are too young to separate from their mother and then Francie III is expecting again any day now.''

Duke was astounded by the casual recitation. ''Just how many kittens are we talking about? I mean at your house, not in the car.''

''Well, of course, there's no way of telling for sure with Francie, but I think there were five, maybe six others when I left, plus the mothers and a tomcat.''

''You can't even keep track of the number of cats living with you?''

''It changes, you see. Sometimes a neighbor's tomcat will just wander in and make himself at home, which probably explains why there are so many kittens in the first place. And people find strays and drop them off on my doorstep. I never quite know what to expect.''

"You're a vet. Couldn't you stop this?"

"I would, but people know I love cats, so they're always coming to me when they want one. Sometimes they're just not adopted as quickly as I would like, but sooner or later they all wind up in good homes." She smiled winningly again. "Like yours. This would be an excellent opportunity for the boys to prove to you that they can take responsibility for a pet, so you'd get them the puppy they want.''

"And how many puppies do you have around the house?" he inquired suspiciously.

"None. I found they don't get along all that well with the cats. I take those out to Uncle Cody. He's a real sucker for a stray dog.''

"And you think I'd be a sucker for three kittens?"

"Oh, no," she said, sounding genuinely horrified. "I mean the boys did say you were lonely, but..." She winced. "Well, never mind. I just thought maybe you'd be willing to help me out for a bit.''

Duke eyed his sons. Obviously they'd had a big day. They'd turned downright chatty with Dr. Dani. He would have to warn his latest housekeeper not to take them into town again until they turned twenty. Maybe then they would stay out of mischief and keep the details of his personal life to themselves.

"Look, it was really nice of you to come out here, but I'm afraid I'll have to take some time to think about this.''

"But you have to at least look at the kittens," Zachary pleaded. "They're really cute.''

"And they need homes," Joshua added. "Just like we did."

Duke scowled at Dani, annoyed that she'd put him in this position. The boys knew the rules. Apparently, they also knew he would never be able to resist Dani Adams. "Don't you want to chime in with your two cents?" he asked her.

She grinned. "No, they're doing pretty well on their own. I hate to oversell."

He surveyed her thoroughly just to watch the color climb in her cheeks. "Darlin', something tells me you could sell a man just about anything you put your mind to."

To his amusement, she blushed furiously at that, but held her ground.

"About the kittens," she persisted.

Duke recognized that he had been outmaneuvered and outmanned. Heck, he'd been sold when Dani Adams first opened her pretty little mouth. Besides, how much trouble could a kitten get into? "Okay, okay, I'll look at them. But we're just taking one. No more. Is that clear?"

The boys exchanged a look, but nodded dutifully.

Five minutes later, Dr. Dani Adams was tearing down the driveway kicking up dust again, and he and the boys were each holding one squirming kitten. For the life of him he couldn't remember exactly how that had happened. Something told him that a man would have to watch his step every single second around that woman or taking in stray kittens would be the least of his problems.

Back inside, he left the boys playing with the kittens, and headed straight for the kitchen where he could hear Paolina banging around pots and pans in time to the salsa music she was playing loudly enough to wake the dead. He hadn't decided if the woman was hard of hearing or just used the music to drown out his orders and the boys' complaints.

"Paolina?" he shouted over the din. When she didn't respond, he reached out and turned off the huge boom box on the counter. "Paolina?"

She glanced up at him in surprise. "*¿Sí?*"

"Did you drive the boys into town today?"

She tilted her head and regarded him warily as if trying to determine the politically correct response. "*Sí,*" she said eventually. "They ask to go."

"Because of the dead goldfish," Duke said.

She bobbed her head. "*Sí, sí, muy muerto.*"

"Paolina, the next time the boys want you to take them into town, call and check with me first, okay?"

"Call, *sí, sí.* I will call."

He doubted she really understood a word he was saying, but he figured it was worth a shot. Paolina had been recommended by Jordan. She was related somehow to the line of housekeepers that had been working for their family for generations. A distant cousin, Jordan thought. Just here from Mexico. Very legal. All of her papers were in order. She just needed a job and a few basic language lessons, Jordan had promised.

Duke was quickly discovering, however, that if he hoped to have any kind of intelligent conversation with her, he was going to have to brush up on his Spanish. What puzzled him, though, was that she seemed to have no difficulty whatsoever comprehending the boys.

"*Gracias,* Paolina," he finally said with a sigh, hoping that at least some of his message had gotten through.

She smiled brightly. "*De nada, Señor Duke.*"

He retreated to his study, only to find two boys and three rambunctious kittens there before him. The kittens had apparently been on his desk. Papers were scattered in every direction and one kitten, the one they'd informed him was his, was kneading whatever papers remained in his briefcase. Hopefully, it was the contract for those blasted mineral rights Jordan wanted to acquire. He could use the destruction of the paperwork as an excuse to delay the acquisition until he could get more facts to back up his belief that it would be a bad deal.

He nabbed the kitten as he sat down and allowed it to settle in his lap, where it purred contentedly. He found the sound soothing, even though his thoughts were in turmoil. Images of Dani Adams kept flashing through his mind. Those tantalizing flashes pretty much spoiled the head of steam he was trying to work up all over again at her father. He settled back and let the images linger.

She wasn't his type, not really. A little stiff, a little uptight and way, way too brisk and professional. He preferred women who were soft and cuddly and accommodating, the opposite of all those social workers and foster mothers who'd made his childhood a living hell. At least that had been his preference before he'd settled down with Caroline. Since the separation, he'd steered as far away from romantic entanglements as he possibly could. Maybe his type had changed.

Before he could spend too much time contemplating the likelihood of that, his phone rang. He didn't waste his breath trying to shush the twins, just grabbed the portable and walked through the French doors onto his patio.

"Duke? It's Jordan."

His shoulders tensed. "Yes," he said curtly.

"Look, I'm sorry our discussion got out-of-hand earlier. I put you into that position so I could take advantage of your expertise. I should be listening to you."

"With all due respect, yes, sir, you should."

"Still won't cut me any slack, will you?" Jordan said with a laugh. "Even when I'm trying to apologize."

"Sorry. I guess I missed that part."

"Maybe that's because I'm out of practice," his boss conceded. "Look, jot down some of your thoughts and let's go over this again in the morning, okay? Maybe clearer heads will prevail by then."

"Mine or yours?"

"Hopefully, both. My wife says I behaved like an arrogant, pigheaded idiot."

"You'll get no argument from me, sir."

"Kelly said the same thing about you."

Duke chuckled. "No argument there, either. I'll have my reasoning on paper in the morning."

"Good. Now, tell me. How are you and the boys settling in? I should have asked you that earlier today. Do you like it here? Is there anything you need?"

"The boys love it," Duke said.

"But you're still fighting the desire to get back into the field," Jordan guessed.

"Yes," he admitted, knowing that the older man would understand. At one time Jordan had been a wildcatter himself, trying to make a place for himself in a business vastly different from his family's cattle empire.

"You'll find this challenging enough in time," Jordan promised. "I'll see to it."

If Jordan didn't, Duke had a feeling his daughter could. "By the way, I met your daughter today," he said.

"Dani?" Jordan asked, clearly surprised. "How'd that happen?"

He related a condensed version of the dead goldfish saga that had his boss laughing.

"So how many kittens did she stick you with?" Jordan asked before Duke had even gotten to that part.

"Are you psychic or something? How did you know about the kittens?"

"Son, from the day I married her mother the house has been crawling with kittens, and I'm allergic to the blasted beasts. Dani has a way with her."

"I'll say," Duke muttered.

"Did she pull out the sob story about drowning them in the river if no one took them?"

"Good God, no."

"That's the one she used on me. Those big eyes of hers filled up with tears. She told me that's what

Kelly intended to do to them unless I agreed to let them stay."

"And you believed her?" Duke asked skeptically.

"Of course not. Kelly's got the softest heart in the universe. But I had to admire Dani's ingenuity. My father bought it, though. She had cats all over White Pines by the time she was six or seven. Somehow over the course of twenty odd years she's managed to convince my father that it's a win-win situation. He saves the cats. The cats keep the mice away."

"Amazing," Duke said, thinking that Harlan Adams's legendary reputation did not include any reference to the notion that he was a soft touch.

"You could have told her no," Jordan pointed out. "You had no problem delivering news I didn't want to hear."

"This was different."

"Yes," Jordan said thoughtfully. "I imagine it was. Good night, son. We'll talk in the morning."

"Good night, sir."

After he'd hung up, Duke had the awful feeling that he'd revealed far more about his reaction to Dani Adams than he'd ever intended. And he didn't like that speculative note he'd heard in Jordan's voice one little bit. It appeared he was going to have to be on his guard about more than business when he went into work in the morning.

And he was going to have to stay the hell away from Dani Adams and her cats. Even as he reached that conclusion, one of those blasted little kittens tried to crawl up the leg of his pants, its claws biting into his flesh even through the fabric. He heard the snag, even before he caught the plaintive meow. Looking down he saw that the kitten was caught partway up his calf.

"You're going to be nothing but trouble," he muttered sourly as he leaned down to disentangle the animal.

But even as he said it, he brought the soft, tiny creature up to curl against his chest.

"Nothing but trouble," he murmured again. This time, though, he was thinking of Dani Adams when he said it.

Chapter Three

Dani was pretty sure she held her breath all the way
back into Los Pinos. Duke Jenkins was the kind of
overwhelming, purely masculine man who made a
woman's toes curl without half trying.

With the notable exception of her stepfather, she'd
spent her whole life around men whose fashion sense
gravitated toward denim. Somehow Duke Jenkins had
managed to make a perfectly respectable business suit
and starched white shirt look as if he were only seconds away from stripping down to nothing. Her imagination had run wild. If a man like that put his mind
to it, he could probably seduce a tree stump.

Of course, there was no chance of him trying anything with her. He worked for Jordan. More impor-
tantly, she was immune to his charms. He was a single dad, which placed him so far off-limits he might

as well have been in Alaska with a barricade around him. With any luck she would never see him or his boys again. With better luck, she would never even hear his name mentioned.

Luck, of course, was never on her side, not when it came to matters of the heart, apparently.

No sooner had she walked into the house than her phone rang.

"I hear you met your father's new vice president today," her mother said without so much as a minute of small talk to disguise her prying.

"How could you possibly have heard a thing like that already? I barely left the man's house an hour ago. Do you have spies over there? Or can I blame this on Grandpa Harlan. I know he has them everywhere. He always knows what we're up to, half the time before we do. It's unnerving."

"You can't blame this one on your grandfather. Jordan spoke with Duke earlier on a business matter. He mentioned that you'd been there. He said you talked him into taking a few kittens off your hands," she reported with obvious amusement. "Jordan said he sounded a little bewildered by how that had happened."

Dani chuckled. "I'm sure Dad could identify with that."

"Indeed. I overheard him sympathizing rather sincerely. He told Duke to watch his step around you or his house would be crawling with all sorts of critters."

"I'm not that bad," Dani protested.

"You'll never convince Jordan of that. He wasn't

the least bit interested in owning one cat, much less the dozens you paraded through here over the years.''

"That was better than my brother's snakes and you know it.''

Her mother laughed. "You bet. I'll tell Jordan to remind Duke of that when he's cussing about the cat hair all over the house.''

She paused and all of Dani's self-protective instincts went on full alert. Her mother turned hesitant only when she knew she was about to tread on dangerous ground.

"So,'' her mother began a little too casually, "what did you think of him?''

"Who?'' she asked just as innocently, determined not to be sucked into making an admission she could never live down. If she so much as hinted that she'd been attracted to Duke, even on a purely physical level, the meddlers in the family would turn that into an engagement before she could blink.

"Duke, of course.''

"I didn't notice.''

"Sweetie, a woman would have to be dead not to notice a man like Duke Jenkins.''

"Okay,'' Dani conceded grudgingly, aware that nothing less than total honesty would satisfy her mother. She might as well get it over with. "If I were to have to give a totally objective description of the man, I'd say he's quite a hunk.''

"An understatement, if ever I've heard one,'' her mother concurred. "He's gorgeous with all that thick, sun-streaked hair and those shoulders...'' She sighed. "My goodness, those shoulders...''

"Mother!"

"Well, I can't help it. He reminds me of Jordan."

"Is Dad aware that you've fallen for his new protégé?"

"Very funny. The only man I've ever fallen for was Jordan and he knows it. Unfortunately, your father knew it, too. It took Jordan a while to figure out he felt the same way, but once he got the message things have worked out rather nicely."

As she spoke, Dani could imagine her mother's soft, nostalgic smile, the one that always came with any mention of Jordan Adams.

"Anyway, enough about that," her mother said briskly. "We were talking about Duke."

"You were talking about Duke," Dani corrected.

"And you were trying to avoid the subject. I was just going to say if any man on earth needs a woman in his life, he does."

Dani had been waiting for this particular hint. It was about as subtle as a swat with a riding crop. "Forget it," she said emphatically.

"Forget what?" her mother inquired innocently.

"I am not now nor will I ever be interested in Duke Jenkins."

"Because of his boys, I imagine."

"Of course, because of the boys. Mother, I really don't want to get into this again. Just forget it, okay? If you feel some sort of matchmaking force coming over you, give Jenny a call. She's older than I am. She's practically an old maid. Besides, she has Grandpa Harlan's tough hide. She could probably handle a man like Duke Jenkins, plus his sons without batting an eye. She needs a little romance in her life. I don't.''

"Danielle..."

"Don't start with the *Danielle*. That always precedes a lecture and I don't need one. It's been a long day and I'm exhausted.''

"But—"

"Bye, Mom. Good to hear from you. Love you.''

"Danielle! Don't you dare hang up on me.''

With only the slightest twinge of regret, Dani ignored her mother's command and slid the receiver firmly back into its cradle. Francie III crawled into her lap, circled twice, then settled down, purring loudly as Dani automatically stroked her under her chin.

Jenny and Duke Jenkins. Now there was a combination to contemplate. Grandpa Harlan's adopted daughter was as potentially volatile as a high school chemistry lab. Unlike Dani, she would be a more than even match for a man like Duke.

Ironically, though, the thought of seeing the two of them together made acid churn in Dani's stomach. If she hadn't known better, she would have labeled the reaction as pure, gut-deep jealousy, which was ridiculous, of course. No single father would ever stir anything more dangerous than the quiet warmth of friendship in her ever again. She wouldn't allow it.

Famous last words, she thought a few days later when she went to White Pines for the annual Fourth of July celebration. There were Duke, Joshua and Zachary right in the thick of things. There was Jenny, beautiful, dark-haired Jenny Runningbear Adams, holding Duke's attention with her animated telling of some Native American lore. Dani wanted to strangle them both, which was hardly the reaction of a disinterested third party.

Everyone—with the exception of her mother and Jordan—claimed to be absolutely stunned that she and Duke had already met. Her grandfather's claim struck her as a little too hearty, a little too determinedly innocent. She didn't trust the man one iota, not when it came to meddling. How Harlan Adams could have heard about the whole kitten incident she had no idea, but she didn't doubt for a second that he knew every detail. Nothing in Los Pinos and especially with his own family escaped his notice.

Nor did she doubt that Duke and the boys were here at his personal invitation. She doubted he'd needed any coaching from her mother on this one. Grandpa Harlan was a romantic, and he wasn't about to rest until everyone he loved was settled down and as content as he was.

"Nice-looking family," her grandfather observed as if he'd gotten a look inside her head. Old as he was, he still moved with an agility and sneakiness that amazed her.

Dani stared straight into his eyes, hoping her unblinking gaze would persuade him that Duke Jenkins was absolutely the last person on her mind.

"Who?" she inquired.

He returned her gaze with a sharp look. "Don't play that game with me, gal. You know perfectly well who I mean. Saw you looking at them just a minute ago.''

''I was just curious about what they were doing here,'' she insisted. ''Usually it's just family here for the Fourth of July picnic.''

''Can't tell around here anymore who's family and who's not,'' Grandpa Harlan grumbled. ''Besides, your daddy's right fond of the boy. Thought I ought to take a look for myself. I have a lot of respect for a man who's all alone and trying to do right by his kids.''

So did Dani. She just didn't want to be any part of the equation. As if he'd read her mind again, her grandfather squeezed her hand, then took off as if someone had lit a fire under him. When she caught sight of Duke heading her way, a can of her favorite soft drink in hand, she understood why.

He offered her the chilled can without explaining how he'd known it was the drink she preferred, then took a sip of his own beer. ''I counted four cats in the barn when I was out there. How many more have you hidden around the place?'' he inquired.

''Oh, I lost count ages ago,'' she said, even though she knew precisely. ''How are the three I left with you?''

''Still alive, which is something to be grateful for, if you ask me.''

''I knew the boys would take good care of them.''

''The boys? Are you kidding? All three of those blasted kittens have taken up residence in my study. When they're hungry, they chase after me. I can't move from one place to another without tripping over one of them.''

There was too much affection laced in with the grumbling for Dani to take his complaints too seriously. ''Won your heart, did they?''

Duke scowled. ''Even if they had, do you think I'd dare tell you?''

There was a teasing glint in his eyes that Dani found just a little too attractive. She opted for a quick change of subject. ''I saw you talking to Jenny when I got here,'' she began.

''Keeping an eye on me, were you?''

''In your dreams, Mr. Jenkins.''

''It's Duke, darlin'. Once you've given a man kittens, you need to be on a first-name basis.''

''Okay, *Duke*,'' she said with deliberate emphasis. ''Isn't Jenny remarkable? Most men fall all over themselves when they meet her.''

''Really?'' He sounded genuinely surprised. ''Guess I'm not most men. I prefer prim little blondes myself.''

Dani felt her cheeks burning. ''Even when they're unavailable?'' she said tightly.

''Especially when they claim they're unavailable,'' he said. ''Makes me wonder why they're hiding from life.''

''I am not hiding from life,'' Dani protested instinctively.

Duke grinned. ''Oh, did you think I was referring to you?''

''Go to hell, Mr. Jenkins,'' she snapped and turned her back on him. Infuriating, insufferable tease, she thought as she marched off, spine straight. She could hear his soft chuckle as she went.

The rest of the afternoon she did everything in her power to avoid him, but no matter where she went, no matter what she did, she could feel his speculative gaze on her.

"Don't look now, but you've made a conquest," her cousin Angela said when she found Dani sitting all alone in a swing on the front porch.

"If discussing Duke Jenkins is the only thing on your mind, go away," Dani retorted.

"Ah, so he's made one, too."

"Angela, I am warning you. If you say one more word about Duke Jenkins, at least in any connection whatsoever with me, I will leave this party right now."

Her cousin's gaze narrowed worriedly. "Are you okay?"

Dani forced a smile. "Just feeling a little pressured, that's all. Don't worry about it. Tell me about you instead. How's life in Montana? Are you happy?"

Angela sat beside her and set the swing into a lazy motion. "Deliriously happy," she confessed, beaming. "Clint's the most wonderful, sexiest, kindest man on earth. He's the best husband and father a woman could ask for."

Dani chuckled at the exuberant praise. "I seem to recall a time when you thought he was a sneaky, low-down, conniving son of a gun. Are we talking about the same man?"

Angela grinned. "You bet." She regarded Dani

slyly. "Which just proves how quickly attitudes change. Never say never, when it comes to a man."

Dani stood up abruptly. "I have to go."

Her cousin nabbed her hand and held it tightly, preventing the escape. "Dani, I'm sorry. I was just teasing. You know how I am. I didn't realize it would upset you so."

"Never mind." She squeezed Angela's hand reassuringly. "It's okay. I'm too sensitive."

"Maybe if you or somebody would tell me what happened, I wouldn't be sticking my foot in my mouth every time I turn around. My mother, your father, Jenny, practically everyone has told me to leave it alone, but I can't. I care too much about you."

Dani sighed and sat back down in the swing, idly setting it into motion again. "It's not as if it's a big secret," she said finally. "Everyone in the family knows."

"And everyone tries to protect you by being tight-lipped about it, giving you your space," Angela guessed. "Maybe what you really need is to talk about it, scream, rant and rave, get it out of your system."

Dani grinned at the image of herself screaming, ranting and raving. It just wasn't the way she handled things. She kept her emotions all bottled up inside, unlike the rest of her far more demonstrative relatives. She had envied Angela for some of the shouting matches she and Clint had had. Blowing off steam had seemed to pave the way to healing. Maybe her way just allowed the wound to fester.

She'd said absolutely nothing about the broken relationship and shattered dreams when she'd come home to Los Pinos, after leaving Rob. Her family had seen her with him and the girls often enough to know exactly how much she had loved them all. They had come to adore Robin and Amy as well, though her father especially had always seemed to have reservations about Rob. At any rate, they had been able to guess the depth of her anguish and had left her alone to deal with it in her own way.

She glanced at Angela, saw the sympathy and concern in her cousin's expression and decided it wouldn't hurt to just tell her what had happened. Maybe it would put an end to these awkward moments that kept cropping up between them after so many years of being as close as sisters. She would keep the telling simple and dispassionate.

Once she began, though, the words began to pour out, words filled with far more rage than she imagined she had ever held inside.

"That beast, that terrible, awful beast," Angela said fiercely when Dani was done. "How could he do that to you, to them?"

"Relationships don't always work out," Dani said objectively. "I mean now that I think about it, I can see how wrong we were for each other. Marriage would have been a disaster."

"But what about those girls of his? Didn't he take their feelings into account at all?"

Dani found herself trying to defend Rob's decision to go along with Tiffany's demand for a clean break, but she simply couldn't muster any conviction.

"The man was a bastard," Angela said. "Admit it."

"Yes," Dani said softly. "Yes, he was."

"A little louder. I didn't quite hear that."

"He was a lousy, good-for-nothing, son of a bitch."

Angela grinned. "Better. Want to try one more time?"

Tears rolled down her cheeks, but she shouted the words at full volume, adding a few more derogatory remarks for good measure. It was surprisingly cathartic, she concluded, laughing.

"I hope you weren't talking about me," Duke said, appearing out of nowhere at the end of the porch.

Dani couldn't seem to find her tongue, but Angela grinned at him.

"Is that how people usually refer to you, Duke?"

"Some do," he admitted.

"Well, you can rest easy. In this case, we were talking about someone else."

His gaze settled on Dani, his expression thoughtful. "I see."

Angela looked from Dani to Duke and back again. "I think I'll run along now. Clint's probably wondering where I disappeared to. He gets panicky when he thinks he's going to have to change a diaper."

Something that felt a whole lot like panic settled in the pit of Dani's stomach as well as she watched her cousin disappear and saw Duke striding up onto the porch. She hadn't realized she was holding her breath until she felt it slowly expel when he settled against the railing opposite her, rather than in the swing beside her.

"I've been looking for you," he said.

"Why?"

"Just looking for a friendly face."

"And you came looking for me?" she asked skeptically.

"Darlin', you're too polite not to manage a friendly face for a business associate of your father's. Besides, you want me to keep those kittens, don't you? You're not going to risk offending me."

"I'm sure Jenny—"

"I've talked to Jenny. I've talked to everyone here. I'd rather just hang out here with you for a while, if you don't mind."

"And if I do?"

"Then I'll leave."

Her gaze narrowed. "Would you really?"

"Absolutely." He grinned. "But I'd be back."

Dani sighed wearily. "Don't tell me you're the kind of man who only wants what he can't have."

"Are you saying you're not interested?"

"I believe I told you once today that I'm not available."

"Because of that jerk you were cussing out when I turned up?"

Oh, God, he had heard. "How much did you hear?" she asked, flushed with embarrassment.

"Enough to know you've been badly burned, that you're gun-shy."

She forced herself to meet his gaze evenly. "I've been around guns all my life. They don't scare me."

"Was that meant to be a warning?"

"Just stating a fact."

"Duly noted, then. Which brings us back to you and me."

"There is no you and me," she said impatiently. "Not today, not tomorrow, not ever."

He didn't seem impressed by her declaration. "Bet I could change your mind," he said.

"You'd lose."

His gaze locked with hers and made her tremble, proving his point. Hopefully, though, he hadn't noticed.

"Wanna bet?" he said softly.

Before she could guess what he intended, he'd clasped her hands and pulled her to her feet. In less time than it took to blink, she was in his arms and his lips were seeking hers.

When his mouth settled gently over hers, she thought briefly about struggling, about directing a well-aimed blow into someplace that would prove just how serious she was about being left alone. The thought vanished before she could act on it, lost to a sea of sensations so sweet, so wildly erotic that her knees went weak and all she could do was cling.

An aching need began to build inside her. Slowly she slid her hands into his thick, silky hair and opened her mouth to the endless, provocative kiss.

It might have gone on forever. She certainly wanted it to and Duke showed no signs of relaxing his embrace. It was the sound of voices nearby that forced them apart, both of them breathing hard and looking dazed. She was pleased to see that he looked at least as shell-shocked as she felt.

That was her ego talking, of course. When she managed to get her brain functioning again, she re-

alized that she didn't want him getting any crazy
ideas from that kiss. One kiss, well, that was just a
kiss. It didn't have to lead to anything more. It
couldn't lead to anything more.

If she'd doubted that for an instant, the sight of his
sons barreling around the corner of the house at full
throttle, shouting for him at the top of their lungs
would have convinced her. They were cute kids, wonderful, exuberant kids. Duke was quite obviously a
great father. There was no room for her in that mix.
She wouldn't risk it for the boys. She didn't dare risk
it for her own peace of mind, either.

"Dad, we've been looking everywhere for you,"
Zack shouted.

"And why is that?" Duke asked, his hand dis-
creetly but possessively resting on her waist.

"It's time for the fireworks," Joshua explained, excitement sparkling in his eyes. "Can you believe it?
They're going to have their own show right here.
Grandpa Harlan—he said we could call him that—he
said we could sit with him and the guy who sets them
off and see how they work. Come with us, okay?"

"You run along," Duke said. "I'll be there in a
minute. If they start before I get there, do not touch
anything. Understood?"

"Okay," they chorused. The two boys regarded
him worriedly. "You will be there in just a minute,
right? Promise? I don't think they'll wait forever. It's
almost dark now."

"I promise."

When they'd gone, Duke drew Dani back around
to face him. "Come with me."

She shook her head. "No, you go. Share this with

your boys. Obviously, they can't wait to see the fireworks with you."

"I don't think they'd mind sharing them with you, too. In fact, once the show begins, I doubt they'll even know I'm around."

"Please," she said. "Just go."

He regarded her with concern. "Dani, do we need to talk about what just happened here?"

"Nothing happened," she insisted.

"If you believe that, we don't need to talk, we need another demonstration."

She held him off this time, just as she should have done the first time he bent toward her. To her relief, he didn't argue. He released her slowly, then trailed his knuckles gently down her cheek.

"Later, then," he said, proving that it was only a temporary reprieve from the storm of emotions he'd set off inside her. He tucked a finger under her chin and lifted it until their gazes were even. "No fireworks could possibly match the sparkle in your eyes, darlin'. Remember that, okay? Remember, too, that I'm the one who put it there."

Remember it? Dani thought it was quite possibly the most romantic, most dangerously seductive thing any man had ever said to her.

Her sigh was heavy and filled with regret. She was going to have to work very, very hard to pretend she'd never heard him.

Chapter Four

Duke could still feel the tentative movement of Dani's mouth under his, could still feel the shudder washing through her body and the sweep of her fingers through his hair when she finally surrendered to that Fourth of July kiss. The memories alone were enough to leave him hot and cranky with frustrated longing.

He'd never experienced such an instantaneous response to a woman before, at least not one that posed so many complicated risks. Attraction was one thing. He appreciated a beautiful woman as well as the next man. But what he'd felt during that impulsive kiss had unexpectedly rocked him, touched him on another level.

The kiss had been a mistake, a terrible, dangerous mistake, he concluded. She was clearly vulnerable.

She was his boss's daughter. He was in no position to, had no desire to, get serious with any woman. He was barely coping with a new job and being a full-time father. Adding a woman to that would just beg for disaster. The list of sensible reasons to stay the hell away from her went on and on.

Yet he knew himself well enough to realize that if the chance came, danger or no danger, he would take it again. She was as intriguing to him as a hint of oil beneath the earth, as alluring as the elusive scent of crude just out of reach.

He smiled at the thought. Dani might be a practical, no-nonsense kind of woman, but he doubted she would appreciate being compared to the search for an oil well. Yet for him nothing was more magnificent, more compelling than that particular hunt. Nothing got his juices flowing quicker than an oil strike.

Nothing except sex, of course. The thought of heated bodies and pleasurable sex brought him full circle, straight back to Dani. That totally uninhibited kiss had told him that Dani's prim facade would disappear in bed. He wanted to make that happen. He wanted to watch the transformation, the flaring of passion in her eyes, the hardening of her nipples, the restless writhing of her slender, normally controlled body.

"Duke?" Lizzy Adams peeked around the edge of his door. "Jordan's looking for you."

He shook off his daze and stared. He could feel a sheen of perspiration forming on his brow, but resisted the urge to mop it off.

"Why didn't you buzz me?" he inquired testily.

Rather than taking offense at his tone, she grinned. "I have been," she said. "For the past five minutes." She regarded him speculatively. "I guess you were lost in thought. Thinking about Dani, I'll bet."

Apparently, all of the Adams women were mind readers, he concluded, scowling at Harlan's precious daughter, who was also Jordan's baby sister. She was still in school and already so sexually precocious it was scary. She flirted with him outrageously or at least she had until she'd seen him with Dani at the family's Fourth of July gathering. All day today she had merely regarded him with very grown-up amusement.

As he tried to gather his composure, he told himself he would be very glad when Lizzy went back to school in the fall and he got himself a real secretary. An *old* secretary, he amended. He wasn't worried that the replacement would have as sassy a tongue. No one who wasn't an Adams would dare to take the liberties Lizzy did when it came to bullying her boss and meddling in his affairs. That particular trait seemed to come with the Adams genes.

"Tell Jordan I'll be right there."

"Already told him. That was five minutes ago, though. You're already late."

"Any idea what's on his mind?"

"Sure. He wants to know if you're interested in Dani." She shot him another unrepentant grin. "We all do."

"It's none of your business," he grumbled as he passed her. "Remember that."

She regarded him worriedly. "Can I give you just the teensiest piece of advice?"

"Can I stop you?"

"Don't try telling that to Jordan. He's just like our dad. They both figure it's their God-given right to meddle in everyone's life."

"Not mine," Duke said succinctly.

"Unless it happens to cross paths with Dani's," Lizzy pointed out, then shrugged. "I say go for it, though. She's been sad for way too long. She needs somebody to shake her up, make her forget about that creep who dumped on her. Something tells me nobody could do that better than you. There's not a woman on the premises who doesn't swoon when you pass by."

"I'm delighted to have your blessing," he said dryly. "Unfortunately, it appears that's not the one I need."

"It's a start," she retorted cheerfully. "Good luck."

Duke took his time walking down the short executive suite corridor to Jordan's office. If he had his way, they wouldn't have this conversation. Unfortunately, it appeared unlikely that he was going to get his way, which meant he'd better come up with some satisfactory answers for the questions Jordan was likely to ask.

In typical fashion, his boss didn't waste time on small talk. Duke was barely across the threshold when Jordan scowled at him and asked, "What's going on between you and my daughter?"

Duke took his time responding. He deliberately

sprawled in a chair opposite Jordan, hoping that the casual pose would communicate in a way that words could not that he wasn't going to be intimidated. Eventually, he shrugged. "Nothing as far as I know. Have you asked her?"

Unfortunately, Jordan was too sharp a businessman to be fooled by Duke's tactic. "Oh, please, don't give me that," he shot right back. "I want a straight answer."

Duke sat up a little straighter. He met Jordan's gaze evenly. "I don't know what you've heard, sir, but that's the truth. We've barely met. She's made it plain she's not interested. What more is there to say?"

To Duke's astonishment, Jordan actually chuckled at that. "I don't suppose you see the contradiction in that, do you? According to your claim, you two hardly know each other, but already she's felt it necessary to tell you she's not interested. What do you suppose brought that on? You don't expect me to believe it's how she opens every conversation with a man, do you?"

He flinched at the direct hit. "I suppose not."

"Could it have something to do with you kissing her the other night?"

Duke stared. "How the hell do you know about that?"

Jordan almost looked as if he felt sorry for him. "Son, you were on the front porch of my father's house in the middle of a family picnic. The teenagers sneak around like budding operatives for the CIA. You can't keep a secret with this clan if you bury it in a cave a thousand miles away. How do you expect to keep anything quiet when you're right in the thick of things?''

''A good point,'' Duke conceded. ''I'll have to be more careful next time.''

Jordan looked positively hopeful. ''Then there's going to be a next time?''

Duke gave up on the evasions. ''If I have my way,'' he admitted.

Jordan gave a little nod of satisfaction. ''Good.'' He studied Duke intently. ''Dani's had a rough time these past couple of years ever since she broke up with her fiancé, Rob Hilliard. If I'd been more on top of things, maybe I could have done something to save her all that heartache.'' He sighed with obvious regret, then looked directly into Duke's eyes. ''It won't be easy getting her to trust you, you know that, don't you?''

''Nothing worth having ever is.''

''Yes, you of all people would know that, wouldn't you?''

''Then I have your approval to keep seeing her?''

''Would it matter if you didn't?''

Duke met Jordan's gaze with a steady, unblinking look of his own. ''No, sir. With all due respect, it wouldn't.''

''That's what I thought,'' he said, sounding pleased. ''Just one thing, though.''

''Yes?''

''Hurt her and there won't be a place on earth you can hide.''

''Understood.''

* * *

Contriving to see Dani again was a whole lot simpler than Duke had anticipated. He should have realized that a powerful man like Jordan wouldn't be content to sit on the sidelines and let things unfold at their own pace. Less than an hour after their conversation, Duke had an invitation to dinner the next night.

"Nothing fancy. Just the five of us," Kelly Adams told him.

"Five?"

"Jordan and I, you and Justin. And Dani will be here, of course."

Of course, he thought. "I'll give her a call and offer her a lift," he said. He cursed the eager note that had crept into his voice.

"I wouldn't, if I were you."

Damn, did everyone in this family meddle? "And why is that?" he inquired.

"She doesn't exactly know you're coming," Kelly confessed.

"And you think if she knew she'd find an excuse not to come," he concluded.

"I'd say that's a safe bet. You unsettle her," Kelly said. "I could see that at the picnic. Now me, I think that's a good thing. Dani wouldn't."

Duke didn't like it, but he could see the wisdom in taking Kelly Adams's advice. He doubted anyone knew Dani as well as her own mother. He supposed there was something to be said for the element of surprise. In fact, he couldn't wait to see the expression on her face when she realized they'd been thrown together again.

"I see," he said blandly. "Well, if you think that's best."

"I do. Of course, you could hitch a ride over here with Jordan," she suggested slyly.

"But then I'd have to get a ride home," he protested, then smiled. "Ah, yes, with Dani, of course."

"It was just a thought," Kelly said.

"A good one, too. I'll speak to Jordan and I'll see you tomorrow night."

Jordan didn't bat an eye the next morning when Duke asked for a ride. Duke didn't bother wasting time with excuses. They both knew exactly what the scheme was all about.

"I'll pick you up on my way home from the office," Jordan said. "Do you want a head start so you can change?"

Duke nodded. "A half hour ought to suffice."

"Perfect. I'll clean up some paperwork before I leave."

Duke knew Jordan well enough to realize that even a casual family get-together wouldn't mean blue jeans and chambray. The man had impeccable style and seemed happier in a well-tailored business suit than any man Duke had ever met. Under the watchful supervision of the twins, he finally settled for a pair of slacks from the new wardrobe he'd been forced to acquire for his new executive position. He added a pale blue dress shirt with the sleeves rolled up and the collar open.

Joshua and Zachary surveyed him intently, then

nodded their approval. They didn't seem the least bit disappointed at being left behind, which meant they'd probably cooked up some scheme for getting into mischief.

"You need some of that smelly stuff, though," Joshua advised. "Girls like that."

"I don't," Duke said.

"But, Dad—"

"I am not taking advice from an eight-year-old. You two go and do your homework."

"Can we stay up until you get home?" Zachary asked hopefully.

"Not a chance. I've told Paolina you're to be in bed by nine-thirty."

The twins exchanged a look that suggested they considered Paolina an easy mark. "And if I don't find the two of you in bed and sound asleep when I get back, you'll be grounded until you're twelve," Duke warned.

"Aw, Dad, you wouldn't do that," Joshua said.

"You wouldn't, would you?" Zachary asked more worriedly.

"Don't test me and find out," he warned, scooping them up one at a time for hugs. Moments like this made him realize how much he'd missed during all the times he'd been away.

"Tell Dani hi for us," they shouted after him.

"Tell her the kittens are really cool," Zachary added. "We might not need a puppy, after all."

"I'll definitely tell her that," Duke said just as he heard Jordan tap his horn out front.

To Duke's relief, they spent the ride discussing

business and other impersonal topics. As always, Duke admired Jordan's quick intelligence and shrewd judgment. There was a rock-solid dependability about him that Duke envied. He hoped he could find some way to emulate it and give his sons the role model they deserved.

It took less than a half hour to reach Jordan's property. As they approached the house, Duke surveyed the small place with its colorful garden with some surprise. Huge pots on the porch spilled over with lush, vivid flowers. He had expected Jordan to own something far more pretentious than this tidy, homey farmhouse. Not even a fresh coat of paint could disguise the fact that it was quite old and had never been much more than a struggling ranch.

Only after he was inside did he see that first appearances were deceiving. When Jordan showed him around, he discovered that an addition in the back was spacious enough for an indoor pool, an office with book-lined shelves and a very private master bedroom suite.

Still, the original house was warm and cozy, compared to Harlan Adams's far more formal White Pines. Jordan observed his reaction.

"Not what you expected, is it?"

Duke regretted being so transparent. "Sorry, but no. It's lovely, but I thought you would live in something very modern."

"Modern and pretentious," Kelly chimed in. "He did," she announced as she joined them with a tray of appetizers hot from the oven. "In Houston." She shuddered. "It was awful. Cold, sterile and big enough to house a family of twenty." She brushed a kiss across her husband's cheek. "I convinced him he needed a home, not a showplace."

"She was right, too," Jordan said. "As usual."

"This ranch had belonged to my family for years."

"Kelly single-handedly saved it from ruin after they were gone," Jordan said with obvious pride.

The sound of a car skidding to a halt out front interrupted their conversation. Kelly winced.

"Dani's here," Jordan guessed.

"She drives like you," Kelly complained. "She's going to get herself killed one of these days."

"I haven't," Jordan pointed out.

Duke gathered it was an old argument. He felt his shoulders tense as he waited for Dani to appear. The front door slammed, she shouted a greeting, then came to an abrupt halt at the sight of him. Her smile faded.

Kelly quickly hugged her and whispered something that had Dani managing a tight smile.

"Hello, again," she said tersely to Duke as she bent to give Jordan a peck on the cheek.

"You're looking especially lovely tonight," Duke commented, grinning at the blush that climbed into her cheeks.

"I just came from the Holcombe place. Their dog was having a difficult time delivering its pups. If I'd known there was going to be anyone here beside family, I would have gone home first to change," she said defensively.

"No need to gussy up on my account," Duke said.

"Well, there is on mine," Jordan said, wrinkling his nose distastefully. "You smell like a barn."

"Maybe I should just leave," she said, turning for the front door at little too eagerly.

"Of course, you're not leaving," Kelly said. "You have clothes in your room here."

Dani sighed. "Fine. I'll be back in a few minutes. Where's Justin, by the way? I need to talk to him about something."

"He should be home shortly. He's over at Cody's with Harlan Patrick. Or so he claims. I suspect they're in town chasing girls."

Dani grinned at that. "Having his sister working at Dolan's must really cramp Harlan Patrick's style."

"You should hear Justin on that subject," Kelly said. "He says Sharon Lynn is personally ruining any chance they have of ever getting a date."

"So Dolan's is the hangout for teenagers?" Duke asked.

"It has been for years," Jordan told him. "Not even the fancy new burger franchise that opened up outside of town can compete."

"Thank goodness," Kelly said. "I'm glad my kids didn't grow up with their social lives revolving around fast food and malls."

"If Jenny had had her way, we would have," Dani said. "She's still itching to get a Bloomingdale's close by."

"She just says that to get your grandfather stirred up," Kelly said, then turned to explain to Duke, "It's an old joke between them that she's going to put a

68 NATURAL BORN TROUBLE

mall on his land as soon as she inherits her part of it.''

"We'll see," Dani said. She stared hard at Duke. "I suppose you miss all the fancy Houston stores.''

"Afraid not. Shopping was never my thing. As long as I can buy a good pair of jeans, I'm a happy man.''

Her gaze swept over his clothes, which were far more expensive than even a pair of designer denim pants. "Jeans?'' she said skeptically.

"Darlin', even those of us who hung out around oil rigs know enough to get gussied up for dinner with the boss.''

Jordan and Kelly fought unsuccessfully to hide their grins. Dani frowned at all three of them.

"Since I appear to be the one who's underdressed, I'll go now and spruce up," she said. "I had no idea we were standing on formalities around here these days.''

"Just get the straw out of your hair," Duke taunted, chuckling when her hand flew up in search of the nonexistent piece of straw.

Dani left the room with a scowl, but at least it appeared she didn't head straight for the front door. He glanced at Jordan just in time to see him exchanging an amused look with his wife.

"I think that went rather well, don't you?'' Kelly said.

"The house is still standing, if that's what you mean," Jordan observed dryly.

"I gather Dani is not too keen on surprises," Duke said.

"Not if there's a man involved," Kelly told him.

"I can still skedaddle on out of here, so you all can have a pleasant, family dinner," Duke offered, albeit reluctantly. He doubted he would have made the suggestion if he weren't fairly certain it would be refused.

"No way," Kelly said. "I haven't looked forward to an evening this much in a long time."

"Me, either," Jordan said.

"I'm so glad to be able to provide you both with so much entertainment."

"Don't you worry about entertaining us. Just liven things up for Dani," Kelly said.

Something in her tone alerted Duke to the possibility that she and Jordan were putting a little too much trust in him. They had clearly assumed that his intentions were thoroughly honorable and that they would inevitably lead to something serious developing between him and their daughter. Was that what he wanted? He shuddered at the very thought of walking down the aisle again. He was far from averse to romance, but beyond that? No way.

Which meant, of course, that he was playing with fire here. Perversely, of course, the thought got his adrenaline pumping.

When Dani returned wearing a pair of snug-fitting pants and a cotton blouse, his pulse ricocheted like a bullet glancing off a fence post. She had scooped her blond hair into a careless knot on top of her head, leaving several wayward curls to skim her cheeks and shoulders. Duke felt an almost irresistible urge to tuck each one back into place...or to release the rest and run his fingers through the shimmering golden silk. It was a toss-up which way he'd go, if he had the opportunity.

Thankfully, he supposed, he didn't have to make the choice. Kelly announced that dinner was ready and they all retreated to the dining room. Though Justin hadn't come in, a place had been set for him, which gave Dani the perfect opportunity to sit opposite Duke, rather than beside him as her folks had so clearly intended.

As she slid into the chair, Duke grinned at her knowingly, bringing another of those easy blushes to her cheeks. He discovered he could easily become addicted to watching the color bloom on her pale flesh. Most women he knew were way beyond such easy embarrassment. At the same time, Duke realized that Dani's particular brand of innocence stirred an unfamiliar protective instinct in him. He managed to get through the entire meal without deliberately baiting her.

He was less successful on the ride home. Dani was clearly peeved about being forced to offer him a lift. Her testiness aroused his contrariness. He settled back in the passenger seat and studied her with blatant masculine approval. There was no mistaking the unsettling effect his gaze was having on her. She was shifting gears so furiously that it was a wonder the transmission didn't shriek to a complete stop in protest.

"Dani?" Duke said quietly after a particularly nasty sequence of shifts.

"What?"

"If you don't settle down, we're going to end up in a ditch."

"If you don't like the way I drive, you could always walk."

"And have you feeling guilty for a week for leaving me on a deserted stretch of highway in the middle of the night? I couldn't possibly do that."

"I wouldn't feel guilty," she claimed.

"Yes, you would. Why don't you tell me what has you in such a rotten mood?"

"My mood is just dandy, thank you very much. If you don't like it..."

Duke grinned in the darkness. "I know, I can walk."

"Exactly."

"You aren't by any chance a little peeved that your parents didn't mention I was coming to dinner tonight, are you?"

"It's their house. They can invite anyone they want."

"True, but you're feeling as if you were set up, correct?"

She sighed. "Look, it's nothing against you, really."

"It's just that you're feeling cornered."

"Something like that."

"Why? It was dinner. It's not a big deal."

She actually gave a tight little laugh at that. "Maybe not to you, but believe me, they're hearing wedding bells. They hear them if there's an available man within a hundred-mile radius."

"Don't all parents want to see their children happily married?"

"Yes, but not all of them consider it their personal mission to make it happen. It's embarrassing."

"It shouldn't be," Duke consoled her. "I'm not feeling any pressure here. You shouldn't, either."

"Yeah, right."

"I'm not. Let's make a pact."

She glanced over at him, her expression wary. "What sort of a pact?"

"To stop worrying about what other people think and just see where things take us."

"*Things,* as you put it, aren't going to take us anywhere. I'm not interested."

"So you've said."

"You don't believe me?"

"No, darlin', afraid not."

She shifted gears with another screech, then sped up to something close to eighty. Duke gathered she hadn't liked his response.

"Are you planning on killing both of us just because you don't like hearing the truth?" he inquired. "Or were you just hoping to put the fear of God into me?"

She regarded him hopefully. "Are you scared?"

"Of you? Never."

"Well, you should be," she said testily. "One word to my father that I find you reprehensible and you'd be out of the oil business, not just his, but any oil company."

Duke laughed at the threat. "You think so?"

"I know so."

"Darlin', before you go spouting off idle threats, maybe you should think again about whose idea this little dinner party tonight was."

She fell silent at the reminder. After a moment, she sighed. "Well, hell."

"Come on, Dani. It's not that bad, is it? Nothing has to happen here that we don't want to happen. We're both adults. I've been able to control my libidinous urges for some time now. Something tells me you have, too."

"What's your point?"

"We shared one kiss. The world didn't come to an end, did it?"

"I suppose not," she conceded grudgingly.

"We stopped with just one."

"Only because we were interrupted by your kids."

As soon as the words slipped out, she muttered a curse that had Duke grinning. Wisely, he kept his mouth shut about her very revealing remark.

When she pulled to a stop in front of his house, he made no move to exit. He held out his hand.

"Friends?"

She eyed his hand warily, then eventually reached over and clasped it.

"Friends," she agreed.

The minute her soft skin brushed his, Duke regretted suggesting something as uncomplicated as friendship. It would never work. He wanted her with a ferocity that startled him. If an innocent touch could set off such demanding need, he was in deep trouble. They both were.

He met her gaze and saw that she had reached the

same conclusion. Her eyes had widened with surprise. Then, even as he gazed into them, they darkened with worry.

"Well, hell," she muttered, then carefully withdrew her hand from his. She squared her shoulders with just a touch of defiance.

"Friends," she repeated pointedly. "You promised."

He nodded and after one final look deep into her eyes, he climbed out of the car. Without a goodbye, she shifted very carefully into gear and drove away.

Duke figured he was going to have a lot of very restless nights in the future to regret that idiotic promise of his. His only consolation was the absolute certainty that Dani was going to be tossing and turning, too.

Chapter Five

More than two weeks went by without Dani seeing any sign of Duke. Nor did she hear a mention of his name. In fact, everyone in the family was so careful to avoid so much as a whisper about Jordan's new employee and his sons that she guessed the silence was deliberate.

Her mother, who usually checked in every morning at some point, hadn't called at all the next day. She never had asked how their ride together the night of the dinner party had gone. Nor had anyone brought up the subject when she'd stopped by the following week or the week after that. It was almost as if they'd conceded that their plot had fizzled.

Of course, they were an incredibly sneaky lot. It was all probably calculated to pique her curiosity. She congratulated herself for not allowing the tactic to work, then sighed at the blatant lie.

The truth was she hadn't been able to get Duke off her mind since their first kiss way back on the Fourth of July. Nor had she been able to forget the feel of his lips on hers, the heat of his body or the purely masculine scent of him. And those sweet, sweet words, comparing the sparkle in her eyes to fireworks kept echoing in her head. It didn't seem to matter that so much time had passed since he'd paid her such an endearing compliment. She doubted she would ever forget it.

Of course, that memory was followed by an echo of his promise that they would become friends and nothing more. She couldn't seem to help feeling just a little disappointed that he'd taken her at her word that that was all she wanted. Why the heck hadn't he just swept her off her feet and made mincemeat of her ridiculous claim to be immune to him? They both knew what a lie it was.

Could it be that he was truly a rarity, an honorable man who stood by his word? Did he intend to back off and leave her completely alone except for chance meetings? That prospect left her feeling thoroughly disgruntled.

"Enough," she said sternly and marched herself into the animal clinic. Work had always been able to dull the most painful memories. Surely it could take her mind off of Duke Jenkins for a few hours. She had a half hour before regular office hours. She would spend it with Honeybunch.

Thankfully, the German shepherd was improving

daily, though it would be another week or two before she felt confident enough of his health to send him back out to Betty Lou's. The old woman had hitched a ride with a neighbor every single day to check on her dog. Dani was fairly confident that it was the sound of Betty Lou's voice as much as her own medical expertise that had kept the dog alive through several touch-and-go incidents.

"Come here, big guy," she called softly. The dog's tail thumped once, and he struggled to his feet. He limped over to the edge of his pen and licked her hand. Dani hunkered down in front of him. "You feeling better? You know, you gave us all quite a scare the night the sheriff brought you in here."

Honeybunch's responding *woof* sounded creaky from disuse.

"No, no, don't apologize. It's not your fault that creep slammed into you," she said as she expertly ran her hands over his body checking his injuries. Everything seemed to be healing nicely. His stitches would come out tomorrow and then it would be mostly a matter of letting him get his strength back. His appetite was slowly returning, and he was regaining some of the weight he'd lost.

"Betty Lou is going to be very glad to get you home again," she told him. "She misses you."

The dog cocked his head at the mention of his mistress's name, then uttered a plaintive woof that had Dani smiling.

"Soon, boy. She'll be here soon," she promised.

"What happened to him?" a familiar male voice inquired, causing her to jump.

She glanced over just as Duke hunkered down beside her, his expression sympathetic as he allowed the dog to lick his hand. He seemed oblivious to the danger of getting dog hair all over his expensive suit. For some reason that pleased her deeply. Nor could she help noticing how strong his hands looked, yet how gently they moved over the injured dog.

"Hit by a drunk driver," she told him.

"Damn fool," he muttered, never taking his eyes off the dog. "I suppose he left the scene, too."

"Of course, but the sheriff caught up with him. A neighbor spotted the car and turned him in. He'd had his license revoked the month before."

"But he was still behind the wheel," Duke said with disgust. "Maybe sooner or later someone will start taking away their cars, instead of their licenses."

"My sentiments exactly," Dani said, standing up and giving Honeybunch a dog biscuit to chew on. She managed to inject a casual note into her voice as she asked, "What brings you by? And how'd you get past Maggie?"

"Is Maggie that perky young lady out front reading a veterinary medicine textbook?"

"That would be the one," Dani said. "Forget I asked. If Maggie was studying, she'd let Martians invade without batting an eye."

"I hope I am somewhat less formidable than Martians," Duke said.

Dani wasn't so certain, so she let the comment slide. "And you're here for?"

"Kitty litter and cat food," he responded easily.

"Mittens and the others go through the stuff faster than the boys go through a gallon of milk."

Dani grinned. "Are you so sure that some of that milk isn't going into the kittens, as well?"

"Now that you mention it, no."

Since the explanation for Duke's presence was so patently flimsy, she couldn't help teasing him about it. "You could have gotten the supplies you wanted at the grocery store, you know. They carry every brand you could want and their prices are much lower than mine."

"But then I wouldn't have had an excuse to see you," he admitted, his gaze settling on her face and lingering until her cheeks flushed.

It was what she'd expected, *hoped*, he would say, but she began a protest just the same. "Duke—"

"I know. I know. You're not interested."

"And you promised—"

"I promised we'd be friends, not that I'd avoid all contact," he pointed out.

"Is that why you've made yourself so scarce the past couple of weeks?" she asked without thinking of the implication of the question.

Naturally, though, Duke didn't miss it. His eyes lit with amusement. "So, you did notice. Good. Actually, I was out of town for several days on business. Jordan could have told you that if you'd asked."

"You've got to be kidding," she said. "Do you know what he'd make of my asking?"

"No more than I am, probably."

Dani scowled at him. "Well, don't let it go to your head. My curiosity was no more significant than if I'd been wondering about the absence of ants at a picnic.''

"Lumping me in with other pests and nuisances?" Duke inquired.

Dani shrugged. "If the shoe fits…"

"A lesser man might be insulted by the comparison and give up. Is that what you're hoping? If so, you might as well save your breath. I'm a persistent kind of guy.''

"Your persistence would pay off a whole lot faster if you picked somebody else to pester," she pointed out.

"Heck, Dani, surely you know that the chase is half the fun.''

She frowned at the flippant words. "You see, that's exactly the problem," she said with gathering intensity. "It's all a game to you. You have two sons. You shouldn't be playing games. In the end they're the ones who'll get hurt.''

His gaze narrowed. "Let me guess. You're talking from experience, aren't you? This has something to do with that jerk, doesn't it? And his kids weren't the only ones who got hurt. You did, too.''

His guesswork was on the money. "It's not important," she insisted anyway.

"Tell that to someone who'll believe it, darlin'. Me, I just figure that gives me an extra obstacle to overcome.''

She found his cavalier attitude exasperating. "Dammit, Duke, there you go again, turning it into some sort of contest. Maybe we can become friends, maybe not, but we sure as heck aren't becoming anything more. Have I made myself clear?''

"Abundantly," he said.

She didn't buy the easy capitulation. "There are a dozen women in this town I could introduce you to this afternoon, who'd be willing to play it your way, no questions asked. Give me the word and I'll call one right now."

"I don't think so," he said, his gaze locked with hers. "There are some obstacles to be overcome, but the fact remains that I've got my eye on you."

She returned his look helplessly. "Why?"

The simple question seemed to stump him as much as it did her. She had to give him credit for considering his answer before he replied.

"Chemistry?" he suggested eventually.

"Chemistry's a whole lot like fire," she warned. "You shouldn't play with it unless you know what you're doing. In this case, way too many people could get burned."

"You could be right," he admitted. "But I've always been a man who liked living on the edge."

"If it were only you and me involved, maybe it would be worth the risk," she conceded.

"It *would* be worth the risk," he retorted emphatically.

Heaven protect her from the male ego, Dani thought. "You and I are not the only ones involved," she reminded him impatiently. "That makes the situation intolerable for me. You're a decent man. Everyone says so. You're doing right by your sons under difficult circumstances."

"Don't make me out to be a saint," he protested.

She grinned at his irritation. "Hardly that." She deliberately reached up and touched his cheek, intent on keeping the gesture as casual as a handshake, as reassuring as a pat on the back. Unfortunately, even that simple contact sent a jolt of pure longing straight through her. She pulled her hand back and jammed it into her pocket, then started briskly down the hall, determined not to let him see how shaken she was.

To her relief, he didn't follow, but his softly spoken taunt did.

"It won't work and you know it," he called after her.

She hesitated, but refused to look over her shoulder. "What?"

"Pretending that there's nothing between us."

She turned then and met his gaze evenly. "There is nothing between us," she said flatly.

He shook his head, a smile on his lips. "Darlin', if you believe that, then I've got a spread of land smack in the middle of a swamp I want to sell you. In fact, I can probably convince you it's suitable for skyscrapers."

When she would have snapped out another retort, he held up his hand. "No, don't say something you'll just have to take back later. I've got time. There's no rush when it comes to romance. In fact, all the experts say slower is better."

He managed to imbue the words with enough seductiveness to set off a stampede of erotic images.

"What happened to friendship?" she asked, fighting the helpless feeling of being caught up in a whirl-wind.

He shrugged. "It's a starting place."

"It's the beginning and the end," she insisted. "Accept that or stop coming around."

He shook his head. "There's that dare again, dar-lin'."

"It's not a blasted dare!" she shouted, then sighed. "Forget it. Obviously, you don't have a clue what I'm all about. Unfortunately, I can read you all too clearly."

"Can you really?" he said doubtfully. He covered the distance between them in three long strides. He framed her face in his hands and settled his mouth over hers before she could blink, swallowing her pro-test.

This time she did fight him. She planted her hands squarely in the middle of his chest and shoved. When that didn't work, she stomped down hard on his foot. He stopped kissing her then, but he didn't release her. He kept his gaze fastened on hers until she was the one who finally sighed and looked away.

"I gather I made my point," he said softly, his thumb caressing her cheek.

"What point would that be?"

"That all the protests in the world won't convince me that there's nothing between us. The evidence says otherwise."

"Believe what you want to. It doesn't matter," she said, forcing herself not to evade his gaze or to react to his touch. "All that matters is that I do not want to become involved with you. Period. End of story."

"I'm sure as an Adams you're used to getting what you want in life," Duke retorted solemnly. "Knowing Jordan, it's probably a family tradition. But I'm afraid you've finally come up against something you can't control."

"Don't be absurd. Of course, I can control it."

"How?" He grinned. "By avoiding me completely?"

"That's one way."

"The obvious one," he said disparagingly. "I would have thought you'd be a little more original, maybe prove yourself under fire, so to speak."

Dani's gaze narrowed. "You are not going to trick me into spending time with you, Duke Jenkins."

He grinned unrepentantly and shrugged. "Ah, well, it was worth a shot. I guess I'll just have to rely on circumstances to throw us together."

"What circumstances?" she asked suspiciously.

"It's a small town. I work for your father. Your family thinks we're a good match. I have three kittens. You're the town vet. Those circumstances."

"You're a manipulative troublemaker, aren't you?"

His booming laugh filled the narrow corridor. "Darlin', coming from an Adams, that sounds a whole lot like the pot calling the kettle black." He pushed open the half-closed door to the waiting room, then paused and winked. "See you around."

"What about the kitty litter and cat food you came in here for?" she blurted.

"Don't worry, darlin'. I'll be back."

A half-dozen speculative gazes followed Duke's

exit. Dani figured it would be less than an hour before the news was all over town that she and Duke Jenkins had had some sort of a lovers' tiff right in the middle of her clinic. Her family would be thrilled.

She, to the contrary, was not thrilled. She was worried. In fact, she was very close to panic. She might not be the most experienced woman on the face of the earth, but she recognized temptation when it was staring her in the face. She was tempted by Duke Jenkins, all right. Trying to convince him otherwise was going to require all her wits and then some. She wasn't even going to bother wasting her energy trying to convince herself.

By the time the clinic closed at five and the last pet, except for Honeybunch, had been shuttled home by its anxious owner, Dani had almost managed to put Duke's visit out of her head. She closed up and wandered down to Dolan's to get a lemonade and a little friendly conversation with Sharon Lynn. Her cousin could always be counted on to brighten her spirits.

Big mistake, she realized when she saw her cousin's eager expression.

"You sit right here and tell me everything," Sharon Lynn said at once, automatically filling a tall glass with ice and lemonade and placing it on the counter in front of Dani.

"Make that to go," Dani said.

"Too late. Come on, spill it."

"The lemonade?"

"Very funny. What exactly happened when Duke came to call today?"

"Nothing happened."

"That's not what I heard."

"Gossip is very unreliable."

"Usually, there's enough truth in it to make it fascinating, though. So, tell the truth, did he kiss you again?"

Dani stared at her in astonishment. "How the heck would anybody know about that? The door was closed."

Sharon Lynn grinned. "So, he did. I suspected as much."

"Are you admitting that you didn't know that already?"

"Well, there was a fair amount of speculation. And Maggie peeked once. She seemed to think she had caught a glimpse of you in his arms."

"I am firing her first thing in the morning," Dani vowed.

"No, you're not. She needs the job and she's good at it. It's not her fault you and Duke decided to get it on in plain sight."

"We did not get it on, as you so charmingly put it."

"But he did kiss you?"

Dani sighed. "Yes."

"And you liked it?"

"No."

"Liar."

"Okay, I liked it, so what? It's not going to happen again. I have made myself very clear on that point."

Sharon Lynn tried unsuccessfully to hold back a grin. "Did you really? Did you by any chance make that same point out at Grandpa's a few weeks ago?"

"Yes, I did."

Sharon Lynn continued to smirk. "Guess he doesn't hear too well."

"He's a man, isn't he? Have you ever known one to listen to a blasted thing we say?"

"Actually, Kyle Mason hangs on every word I say."

"Oh, for heaven's sakes, stop gloating. We all know you caught the last decent man in the universe or so you keep reminding us."

"He is extraordinary, there's no doubt about that. Not that Duke is any slouch. He's charming and sexy and smart."

"How would you know all that? You've barely met the man."

"Not true. He comes in here with his sons all the time." She glanced up. "In fact, they're on their way in right now."

Dani flatly refused to turn around to look. "Please, please, tell me you are making that up."

"Why would I do that?"

"To drive me crazy."

"Not me," Sharon Lynn retorted. "But I'd say someone else is doing a pretty good job of it." Her smile widened. "Hey, Duke. How're you doing? Hi, Joshua, Zack. What's it going to be today?"

"Ice cream cones," Zack replied. "Dad said we could have dessert before dinner tonight. Isn't that cool?"

"Way cool," Sharon Lynn agreed.

Dani felt Duke's hands settle on her shoulders. A shiver skimmed straight down her spine even before he leaned down and whispered, "Told you so."

There was nothing to do but accept the inevitable. Slowly, she swiveled her stool around until she was face-to-face with him. Pure devilment was sparkling in his eyes. His gaze locked with hers and his expression sobered until an exquisite kind of tension shimmered in the air between them. Dani swallowed hard and forced herself to turn away. She smiled at Zachary and Joshua.

"So what's this about dessert before supper?" she asked.

Already licking his double scoop of chocolate ice cream, Joshua paused long enough to say, "Dad says as long as we cross our hearts and promise to eat every bite on our plates, we can do it this way just this once. It's 'cause Dolan's will be closed by the time he finishes fixing dinner."

"Yeah," Zachary chimed in. "It takes him a really, really long time to cook, 'cept when he zaps stuff in the microwave."

"I see."

"Can you cook?" Joshua asked. regarding her speculatively.

"Dani is the very best cook in the entire family," Sharon Lynn said before Dani could respond. "Her spaghetti sauce would bring tears to your eyes. As for her pot roast, well, let's just say that Maritza taught her and Maritza has been Grandpa's housekeeper for practically forever and he has gourmet taste."

Both boys' eyes widened hopefully. "Really? Maybe you could invite us to dinner sometime," Zachary suggested.

"Yeah, we really, really love spaghetti, especially if it doesn't come out of a can," Joshua added.

"Hey, guys, it's not polite to invite yourselves over to someone's house," Duke said.

"Oh, we don't stand on formality around here," Sharon Lynn said. "Do we, Dani?"

Dani gave her a sour look, then forced a smile. "Of course not. The next time I'm doing more than grabbing a sandwich for dinner, I'll give you guys a call."

Duke's eyebrows rose. "A sandwich? That's your idea of a healthy dinner?"

"Sometimes it's all I feel like fixing after a long day."

"Tsk, tsk," Duke chided. "You should know better. I propose that we all go out tonight. My treat. Since everybody's so keen on spaghetti, how's that Italian place? We haven't tried that yet."

"It's the best," Sharon Lynn enthused. "Dani loves their lasagna, don't you, Dani?"

"It's very good," she conceded. "Really, though, I can't. Not tonight."

Duke's gaze clashed with hers. "Busy?"

"Yes."

"Doing?"

She seized on the first thing that came to mind. "I have to keep an eye on Honeybunch."

"Who's Honeybunch?" Zachary asked as chocolate dripped down his shirt. He was oblivious to the melting ice cream. Dani instinctively reached for a napkin and blotted it up, then wiped a streak off his cheek.

"Honeybunch is an injured dog I'm treating," she explained.

"Is he hurt bad?" Joshua asked.

"He's getting better," she conceded.

Duke shot her a triumphant look. "Then we can stop in and check on him on the way to the restaurant. That should put your mind at ease, right?"

She sighed heavily. She might as well give it up. There wasn't an excuse on the face of the earth that would work now, not unless she said flatly that she didn't want to go with them. There were two problems with that one: first, it was rude, second, it was a lie. A huge lie, in fact. She did want to go. Obviously, some part of her didn't care that a situation all too similar to this one had practically destroyed her.

"Why don't I go on ahead while you boys finish your ice cream," she suggested eventually. "You can meet me at the clinic when you're ready."

"Perfect," Duke said. "Fifteen minutes?"

"Yes," she said without enthusiasm.

Sharon Lynn grinned at her. "Have a good evening."

Dani nodded. "I'll speak to you tomorrow," she said, a deliberately dire note in her voice.

"Can't wait," her cousin said, clearly not the least bit repentant over her part in the night's turn of events.

Outside the drugstore, Dani briefly considered bolting, but dismissed it. It would be a cowardly thing to do, and no Adams had ever been a coward. Not that it was Adams blood flowing through her veins, but too many years of the family's influence had had an effect.

Ah, well, she only had to get through the next fifteen minutes of dread and what? Maybe another hour for dinner. An hour and a half, tops. That was hardly an eternity. Nor was it really long enough to feed this ridiculous attraction she was starting to feel toward Duke Jenkins. They would be chaperoned, too.

By ten o'clock she would be home, tucked in bed with a good book, just the way she had been on every single night of the past two years, except for those occasions when she'd been coerced into spending the evening with one family member or another.

The prospect reassured her. She was actually feeling reasonably upbeat when she heard the doorbell ring in the main part of her combination home and clinic. That optimism lasted until the moment she opened the door and saw, not Duke, but Rob, standing on the front stoop.

Chapter Six

Dani stared incredulously at the disheveled man standing on her doorstep. It wasn't so much his identity that shocked her, as his appearance. Rob had always dressed impeccably. Tonight he looked as if he'd grabbed clothes from a laundry basket.

"What are you doing here?" she asked with an icy calm she was far from feeling.

"Can I come in? We need to talk."

"We do not need to talk," she retorted. "And no, you may not come in."

He blinked at her in obvious surprise. "What's the matter with you?"

His total lack of understanding of what he had done to her infuriated her as nothing else could have. Either he was blind or she had been so submissive that he'd anticipated being able to steamroll over her as if nothing had ever happened. Dani didn't like either explanation much. Both said things about her she would rather not have believed true. Well, then, it was about time she stood up for herself and made her feelings perfectly clear.

She stared at him coldly. "That's the problem, Rob. You never did have a clue about anything that mattered. It was always about what you wanted, what you needed."

When she would have slammed the door, he blocked it and for the first time she felt a niggling sense of unease. "Rob, please. Don't make a scene."

"Afraid that shining Adams image will get tarnished?" he asked sourly.

Dani was stunned by his bitterness. What the heck did he have to be bitter about? "Just go away, please. I'm expecting company." She spotted Duke and his sons strolling along the sidewalk less than a block away. "In fact, they're on their way right now."

Rob turned and followed the direction of her gaze. "Still looking for a built-in family, I see. You always were predictable."

Dani winced at the mean-spirited accusation. Any second now rage was going to overcome common sense and she was going to throw a tantrum that would set Los Pinos on its collective backside.

Fortunately, Duke had apparently picked up on the scene even from a distance. He spoke quietly to the boys, who stopped where they were without argument. Then Duke quickened his pace. Before Dani could say anything more, he was casually, but effectively sliding between her and Rob. He dropped a deliberate kiss on her forehead, then fixed an interested stare on her visitor.

"Hey, darlin', who's this?" Duke asked.

"Rob Hilliard. He's an old acquaintance from Dallas."

Duke's gaze narrowed, which suggested he'd heard the name mentioned. Since she'd never told him the identity of the man who'd hurt her, she could only assume that someone else in the family had filled in the blanks she'd left in the story.

"Glad to meet you," Duke said. His tone was polite, but any reasonably bright man would not have found it welcoming.

"Rob was just leaving," Dani prompted, since he appeared not to have taken Duke's hint.

Neither man paid a lick of attention to her. They were squaring off like contestants in a championship boxing match.

Rob was no hero, though. Duke was at least four inches taller and twenty pounds of pure muscle heavier. Eventually her ex-fiancé backed down.

"I'll catch up with you later," he said pointedly to Dani. "Sometime when you're not so busy."

Duke shook his head. "I don't think that's such a good idea," he said. He studied Dani. "Is it?"

"No," she agreed. "It's not a good idea at all."

"Fine. Have it your way." Rob smiled at Dani, but there was little warmth in his expression as he added, "The girls send their love. They miss you."

Dani felt as if she'd been sucker-punched. She could deal with Rob. She could dismiss him as if he

were no more than an inconvenience, but the girls…
She couldn't pretend to be disinterested.

"Are they okay?" she asked.

Rob shot a triumphant smirk at Duke to indicate
his belief that he'd bested the other man, after all.
"They're unhappy."

"Why?"

"As I said, they miss you. They'd like to see you."

The offer was nearly two years too late. Dani didn't
want to ask, but he'd left her no choice. "What about
Tiffany? Won't she object?"

"We split up." Ignoring Duke's presence, he
added, "They want you to come home. We all do."

The thought of holding Robin and Amy in her arms
again, the prospect of reading them bedtime stories
and drying their tears, all of it was almost enough to
make her weaken. Duke's steady hand on her waist
gave her the strength to shake her head. It reminded
her that what she felt for those two darling girls was
not nearly enough to compensate for the fact that their
father was a weak, insensitive fool.

Steeling herself against his likely reaction she said
coolly, "I would love to see the girls again, anytime
you'd like to bring them for a visit. But we will never
be a family, Rob." She met his gaze evenly. "Never.
I'm surprised even you would be foolish enough to
think it possible."

"But…"

"I think you heard her," Duke said quietly. "Now
it's time you were on your way." He glanced at Dani.
"Right?"

"Absolutely," she said.

Only after Rob had turned and walked away, did Dani feel her knees sag. Duke's arm circled her waist protectively. "You okay?" he murmured.

She nodded, unable to speak. There was too much emotion clogging her throat. This time she was the one who'd cut the ties to Robin and Amy, severed them beyond repair. Rob would never bring them for a visit, not now that he knew there was no place for him in her life. He'd been using those poor, sweet babies of his as pawns, just as he always had.

"Josh, Zack," Duke called to the two wide-eyed boys who were still standing where he'd left them. "Why don't you go into the clinic and spend a little time with Honeybunch." He looked at Dani. "Is that okay?"

"Yes," she said. "Just remember he's still hurt. Don't try to touch him."

When they were gone, Duke prodded her into the house. "Sit. Do you want something? Some tea? A stiff drink?"

"Nothing, thanks."

He studied her worriedly. "Are you sure you're okay?"

She managed a faltering smile for him. "Believe it or not, I'm relieved."

He stared at her incredulously. "Relieved? I'm afraid you're going to have to explain that one to me."

"All this time I've worried what would happen if I ever saw him again. At first I prayed that he would come after me, beg my forgiveness and take me back to be a part of his family again, just the way he did tonight.''

''I didn't hear a whole lot of begging,'' Duke pointed out.

''For Rob, what you heard was close enough. Anyway, I imagined myself falling into his arms and going back. It's taken me a long time to realize that I was never half as much in love with him as I was with the girls. I adored his daughters. From the beginning I loved them as much as if they'd been my own.''

She sighed. ''And I worked so hard to win them over. I had Jordan's example to go by. Did you know he once thought he would be a terrible father? He was scared to death of me when he and mom were first seeing each other, but he made me a part of his life just the same. I wanted to make Rob's girls feel just as safe. Tonight when Rob asked me to come back, though, it was like a giant light bulb switching on. I realized I couldn't go just for them. Sooner or later their father and I would have split up and they would be hurt all over again.''

''So all in all, this visit was a good thing?'' Duke asked, his expression skeptical.

''I think so, yes.''

He nodded slowly. ''Okay, I'm glad, then. How the hell did you fall for a weasel like that in the first place?''

Dani grinned at his indignant tone. ''He wasn't at his best tonight.''

''An idiot in sheep's clothing is still an idiot.''

Dani shrugged. ''Much as I hate to admit it, maybe

you're a better judge of character than I am, even if you do play havoc with old clichés. At any rate, Rob no longer matters. Let's eat. Suddenly, I'm starved."

"I do love a woman who has her priorities in order," he said approvingly. "Before we get the boys, though, one last thing."

"What's that?"

"If second thoughts about this Rob person start to sneak up on you in the middle of the night, don't call him," he warned. "Call me. I'll set you straight again before you go and do something rash."

At the moment, Dani couldn't conceive of having second thoughts. Nothing was clearer in her mind than the decision she'd reached just moments earlier to leave the past in the past.

"Promise," Duke insisted, when she hadn't responded.

"I promise," she said. "But—"

"No buts, darlin'. When it comes to love, second thoughts are a given."

"I don't love him anymore," she said with absolute certainty. Relief about that almost left her giddy.

"But you did once. Sometimes, in the middle of the night, that's enough to get you thinking crazy."

She regarded him speculatively. "You've been there?"

"Been there, done that. I don't recommend it."

"Will you tell me about it?"

"Maybe I will," he said. "If you ever make that call to me at three a.m."

Duke had been itching to plant his fist in that Rob person's face from the moment he'd walked up the sidewalk and seen him attempting to intimidate Dani. A thoroughly primitive, possessive instinct had flooded through him, startling him with its intensity. Only the certainty that Dani would have hated the resulting scene had kept him from following through on the urge. Something told him, though, that one of these days he'd get his chance. Men like Hilliard rarely learned their lesson the first time out.

All through dinner he kept his gaze pinned on Dani, watching for signs that she was already having those second thoughts he'd warned her about. She would, too. He'd heard enough to know just how much she'd loved those two kids of Hilliard's. Given the opportunity to have them back in her life, she wouldn't walk away without a single backward glance. The maternal instinct in her ran deep. He'd seen it in her reluctant interaction with Zack and Joshua. Not even past hurts could keep her from treating his sons with genuine warmth. Even now she was asking them about the day camp they were attending and showing the kind of genuine interest that could never be faked.

"Then the lifeguard at the pool said, 'Zachary Jenkins, you get out of the water right this instant,'" Joshua was telling her, his tone mimicking the teenager's precisely. "I said, 'But I'm not Zachary.' She didn't believe me. I got out of the water and five seconds later, Zachary swims smack in front of her. She turned real red and started to yell again, but then she saw me standing next to her. 'Told you so,' I said."

"And what did she do?" Dani asked.

"She said, 'Oh, never mind,' and walked away."

"Interesting story," Duke observed. "What exactly did Zachary do in the first place?"

"Uh-oh," Josh said, a guilty expression replacing the glee with which he'd told the story.

"Told you to keep your big mouth shut," Zack grumbled. "This is payback for the goldfish, isn't it?"

"Is not," Joshua insisted.

"Is, too."

"I'm waiting," Duke said, cutting off the exchange.

"It wasn't anything bad," Joshua said valiantly. "Not really."

"Maybe you should let me decide that," Duke said. "Zack?"

"I just dove into the water," Zack said, his expression totally innocent.

"A cannonball, by any chance?" Duke asked.

"Uh-huh," Josh said, nodding, his eyes alight at the memory. "A real whopper."

"And naturally someone was standing right beside the pool who didn't take kindly to getting splashed from head to toe," Duke guessed. "Who was it?"

"Some old guy," Zack said. "In a suit. Who'd wear a suit to a pool, anyway?"

"The mayor," Dani guessed, not even trying to smother a laugh. "He likes to stop by to see how things are going."

Duke stared at her. "The mayor? Terrific. My boys have been here less than six months, and they've already tried to drown the mayor."

Dani reached over and patted his hand. "Don't

worry. A lot of people in town have considered doing far worse.''

''Then why do they keep electing him?''

''No one else is willing to run.''

''Why? Because everyone knows that it's Harlan Adams who really runs things?'' Duke suggested.

Dani grinned. ''Something like that. Grandpa Harlan does make his opinions known and people do tend to listen to him.''

''Something tells me I ought to send the man a sympathy card,'' Duke said.

''No need to do that. He's heading over here right now,'' she told him, nodding toward the tall, silver-haired man striding purposefully their way. Even from a distance the water spots on his suit were evident.

''Ohmigosh,'' Zachary murmured, sliding down until he was all but under the table.

Duke latched onto his arm and forced him to his feet as he rose himself to greet the older man. Dani's expression suggested she was finding the whole thing just a little too amusing.

''Danielle,'' the mayor said politely. ''Good to see you.''

''Good to see you, too, Frank. Have you met Duke Jenkins and his sons? Duke is a vice president at Dad's oil company.''

If he hadn't been assessing the man so closely, Duke might have missed the subtle shift in his demeanor when he realized that Duke was tied very tightly to the Adams clan. His tone was suddenly deferential and whatever he'd intended to say about the incident at the town pool was swallowed. Duke refused to let his son off so easily.

"I gather you met the boys earlier today," he said. "Zachary, don't you have something you'd like to tell the mayor?"

Zachary looked as if he would rather eat worms, but he dutifully said, "I'm sorry for splashing you, sir. It was an accident."

"Yes, well, a little water never hurt anyone now, did it?" the man said. "Apology accepted."

"Dad, can me and Joshua go play the video games?" Zack asked, clearly anxious to get away before he caused any more mishaps.

"Yes," Duke said, just as eager to have them safely out of the way. He handed them the change he had in his pocket. When they'd gone, he added his own apology for their rambunctious behavior. "And please, let me pay to have your suit cleaned."

"Not necessary," the mayor said. "I just wanted to bring the matter to your attention in case you hadn't heard about it, but I see that wasn't necessary. Good day, Mr. Jenkins. Danielle, give my regards to your father and grandfather."

"Of course," she said, barely containing a chuckle as he walked away.

"What's so amusing?"

"He is. He really didn't have any business wearing a suit and standing beside a pool filled with kids. I swear I think he does it just to get his suit cleaned for free. Guilty parents are easy marks."

Duke stared at her. "This has happened before?"

"Once every week or two as far back as I can

remember. I do believe Justin and Harlan Patrick were guilty of their share of infractions. Dad and Cody finally forbade them from swimming in the town pool. Naturally, that made it all the more fun to go there, even though there's a perfectly good pool at White Pines. They still sneak into town, but they've learned to avoid the days the mayor drops by.''

"You could have told me that before I fell all over myself apologizing,'' Duke grumbled.

"I considered it educational,'' she retorted. "I wanted to see if you were capable of abject humility.''

Duke chuckled despite his annoyance. "Did I pass the test?''

"You were very good. I believed you were very sincere.''

"And the mayor?''

"Once he figured out you worked in an executive capacity for Dad, you could have told him to take a flying leap off the town hall roof and he would have done it and thanked you for suggesting it.''

Duke regarded her speculatively. "You know, Miss Smarty-Pants, it occurs to me that if you hold such disdain for this man, perhaps you ought to run for mayor yourself. At least then the Adams pulling strings around town would be operating in an official elected capacity.''

She looked horrified by the suggestion. "Me? You've got to be kidding.''

"Why not? You're bright. Everyone in town knows and respects you. I think it's a great idea. When's the next election?''

"Thankfully, not for another three years."

"Just long enough to get your campaign funds lined up," Duke said.

Dani's gaze narrowed. "You're teasing me, aren't you?"

Duke shrugged. "A little, maybe. You've been looking a little too serious all evening, despite your claim that your ex-fiancé's appearance didn't upset you."

"It was just a shock, that's all."

"But you can't stop thinking about his girls, can you?"

She smiled sadly. "No."

"Then see them. He's opened the door."

"I can't," she said simply. "It wouldn't be fair to get their hopes up, when I know nothing will ever happen between me and their father. They're used to me being gone now. It's better if it stays that way."

Duke thought back to his own childhood. How many times had he prayed that his parents would suddenly come back to claim him? Even knowing that it was impossible, he'd harbored the dream in some tiny, secret place in his heart.

"They'll never get over losing you," he insisted. "See them. Let them know you still care, even if you can't be with them."

Obviously startled by his vehemence, Dani stared at him. "Experience talking?"

"It doesn't matter," he said. "Just trust me, kids never forget losing someone they love."

"Are you talking about Zack and Joshua? Do they miss their mother so terribly?"

Actually, that had been the farthest thing from Duke's mind, but it was an easier answer than revealing his own childhood traumas. "Of course," he said. "They ask about their mother all the time."

"And what do you tell them?"

"That she was very unhappy with me and that she needed to go away to find happiness."

"Does she stay in touch with them?"

"She did at first. She sent postcards every few weeks. It's been a while now since we last heard from her, though."

Dani reacted with visible anger. "How could a mother do that to her own children? How selfish can she be?"

Duke didn't have any excuses for Caroline, either. It didn't matter to him that she'd seemingly dropped off the face of the earth, but it hurt the boys. He understood that kind of anguish all too well. More than once he'd considered hiring someone to look for her, then dismissed the idea. If she didn't want to be a part of her sons' lives, then forcing her to go through the motions would be worse than letting them grieve and get it over with.

Though he understood its roots, he was still a little surprised by Dani's indignation on their behalf. It reminded him of his very first impression of her. He'd thought then, as he did now, that she would make a terrific mother.

Earlier he'd caught Rob's sarcastic remark that she'd gone looking for another ready-made family. Now he let the idea simmer. It could be a solution for all of them. She would have two boys to replace the girls she'd lost. Joshua and Zack would have a mother's love again. Goodness knew, the pair of them could use a gentling influence.

And him? What would he get out of the bargain? He'd already admitted that he was attracted to her. That was definitely a start. The prospect of having her in his life on a more permanent basis wasn't nearly as distasteful as it probably should have been, given his avowed determination never to marry again.

Years ago no one would have blinked twice at the idea of such a marriage of convenience. Even now there were lonely men in places like Alaska and elsewhere who advertised for mail-order brides. Would this be any different? He found that he was warming to the idea.

He glanced at Dani and saw her staring at the boys wistfully. Yes, he thought again, it would work very nicely for all of them.

"Why don't you go on over there and give them some real competition," he encouraged.

She grinned. "You wouldn't mind?"

"No, indeed. They beat the pants off me. Let them humiliate somebody else for a change."

"Not me," she said, flashing him a smile. "I grew up with a bunch of very competitive relatives. I do believe if you check that particular machine, my record still stands."

Perfect, he thought as he watched her join his sons. Duke was the kind of man who trusted his instincts. He also made decisions in a rush and stuck by them.

For once in his life, though, he managed to curb his enthusiasm. Something told him he'd better have his scheme very well thought out before he presented it to Dani. She struck him as the kind of woman who might not be nearly as pragmatic as he was, even under her own currently vulnerable circumstances. She might prefer at least the pretense of romance.

He could manage that. Hell, she already made him hotter than asphalt in August. A little proper courting wouldn't kill him. Then he could spring the idea of marriage on her and everything would fall tidily into place.

Satisfied with the plan, he sat back in his chair, sipped his beer and observed her. Dani Adams was something, all right. The boys clearly thought so, too.

Now all he had to do was turn up the heat between them a notch or two and his troubles would be over by Christmas, maybe sooner.

All in all, he concluded, the move to Los Pinos wasn't turning out to be quite as miserable as he'd feared. His job might not be as exciting as oil exploration, but courting Dani Adams promised to make up for that.

When she turned toward him, he lifted his mug of beer in a silent toast. Anticipation sizzled through his veins like fine champagne. Yes, indeed, life in Los Pinos promised to get downright fascinating.

Chapter Seven

Getting Dani to fall in with his plans was trickier than riding a bucking bronco, Duke concluded after six weeks of her clever elusiveness. The woman had more unexplained social engagements than anyone he'd ever met. If he hadn't been a confident kind of man, he might have begun to wonder if she wasn't deliberately trying to avoid him. He concluded that he wasn't going to pull off this marriage proposal quite as easily as he'd originally anticipated.

He had surmised very quickly that simply calling and asking for a date wouldn't work. She was way too jittery to accept. She had claimed to be busy every time he gave her any sort of advance notice.

Stopping by the clinic for an impromptu visit was more successful, but he couldn't discuss the future while half her attention was on some kid's parakeet or gerbil.

Finagling invitations from one Adams or another was a snap compared to getting a minute alone with Dani once he was there. If he didn't know better, he would have sworn that she was onto him, that she'd read his mind that night at dinner and resolved to avoid him at any cost.

Of course, that was impossible, he thought as he observed her clean dive into the pool at White Pines on Labor Day. Her swimsuit, modest by current standards, clung to her in a way that made it seem practically indecent. He hadn't been able to tear his gaze away from her since he'd first spotted her emerging, soaking wet, from the pool. A second later she dove back in and remained submerged up to her neck as if to deliberately prevent him from getting another peek at her.

The woman swam like a porpoise and apparently enjoyed it just as much. She hadn't been out of the water all day. Neither had anyone else, which made the huge pool far too crowded for the kind of intimate conversation Duke was interested in having.

"Dani looks happy, doesn't she?" Sharon Lynn observed, perching on the edge of the chaise longue next to him, her expression a little too innocent.

Happy, wet and sexy as hell, Duke would have corrected, but discretion prevented it. He merely nodded. He'd discovered quickly that the only way to avoid prying around this family was to keep his mouth clamped firmly shut. Occasionally, they gave up and went away. Sharon Lynn, unfortunately, showed no such inclination.

"Are you responsible for that?" Dani's cousin inquired in a tone that suggested her interest ran deeper than casual curiosity.

The question might have amused him if it hadn't been so wildly off the mark. "Hardly. I've barely seen her recently." He couldn't help the cranky note that crept into his voice.

"I see," Sharon Lynn said thoughtfully.

"What does that mean?"

"I just thought..." She shrugged. "Oh, well, I guess I was wrong."

"Wrong about what?"

She hesitated as if she were debating with herself. Duke watched the visible struggle with fascination. He wondered what the devil she was hiding...or what she wanted him to think she was hiding.

"Sharon Lynn?" he prodded. "What made you think Dani and I were seeing each other? Has she said something?"

"Oh, no," she said. Again, there was a slight hesitation before she shrugged and said, "It's just that she's been into Dolan's with your sons quite a bit. Almost every afternoon, in fact. I just assumed that ever since you went out to dinner you two were something of an item."

Duke tried to absorb the implication. Dani had been spending time with Zack and Josh? That was news to him. How had this friendship between Dani and his sons developed without his knowledge? Was he that oblivious to the twins' activities or were they deliberately keeping mum about these little get-togethers? Probably the latter, especially if ice cream was involved.

Paolina took them to the town pool every day for swimming lessons, but he'd just assumed they'd gone straight home afterward since he'd all but ordered Paolina not to take them anywhere other than the pool without his specific permission. Naturally, they'd kept quiet about it. They'd known they were breaking the rules.

"What time have they been coming in?" he asked.

"About four, I guess. After their swimming lessons."

It was Duke's turn to mutter, "I see." A few weeks ago he would have grounded them for the infraction, but now he saw that their sneaky little visits could be used to his advantage.

Tomorrow the three of them would have company at Dolan's. Thank goodness school didn't start until the following week or he would have missed out on this opportunity to slip into Dani's schedule when she wasn't expecting him.

He was so busy making his plans, he completely missed the thumbs-up sign Sharon Lynn exchanged with Jenny Runningbear Adams as she strolled away.

"Can't you take a break tomorrow afternoon?" Jenny pleaded with Dani. "I only have a few more days until school starts. We haven't had a long chat since I got back into town."

Dani regarded Jenny suspiciously. "That's right, so

why all of a sudden can't you wait to get together? I have a clinic to run, remember?''

"I know," Jenny said repentantly. "We should have done it sooner. It's my fault. The summer just got completely away from me. You know how I am."

That was the problem. Dani did know. Jenny was one of the most organized women she'd ever met. She didn't fritter away time. She had too much going on.

Like Janet, her mother, Jenny was involved in advocacy programs for Native Americans in addition to her teaching duties. Dani could believe that Jenny hadn't had a second to get together, but she wasn't buying this nonsense about time just slipping away from her. There was a reason for this sudden urgency.

Unfortunately, she couldn't quite figure out what Jenny's angle was. She tried one more time to get a fix on it. "Jenny, why does it have to be tomorrow afternoon? Make it six o'clock and we could have the whole evening. I'll even cook."

"That won't work," Jenny said a little too quickly. "Like I said, school's almost ready to open. I have all my teaching materials to get organized. I don't have another spare minute, especially in the evenings. I've been playing chess with Harlan then. He really looks forward to it."

"So the only time you have free is tomorrow precisely at four?" Dani asked skeptically.

"Yes."

"And I'm supposed to drop everything and meet you and Sharon Lynn at Dolan's for some girl talk? That's all? There's no hidden agenda?"

"Of course not. It'll be fun. I'll even treat."

Dani laid a hand dramatically over her heart. "Goodness, how can I resist an offer like that?"

"Then you'll be there? Four o'clock?"

Dani sighed. The only way she was going to find out what Jenny was up to was to fall in with her plans. "Yes. I'll shuffle some appointments around, and I'll be there."

"Wonderful," Jenny said, then glanced up. "Don't look now, but someone is staring at you. When are you going to give that poor man a break and go out with him?"

"It's not going to happen," Dani insisted.

"But you went out with him once. Didn't you have a good time?"

"That wasn't a date. It just sort of happened."

"Whatever," Jenny said dismissively. "You enjoyed yourself, didn't you? That's what Sharon Lynn said. Your mom said the same thing."

Dani sighed. "I'm glad everyone has been keeping you up-to-date on my activities."

"Were they wrong?"

"No, but I also had a little too much fun hanging out with Duke's kids. I won't take that kind of risk again."

"Because of Robin and Amy," Jenny said.

"And Rob," Dani reminded her. She had told no one about the painful scene over a month ago. She doubted Duke would mention it either.

"Sweetie, something tells me that Duke Jenkins is absolutely nothing like Rob."

Dani had made a similar assessment herself. That still didn't mean she was willing to take any chances with her heart or with his sons'. She'd seen enough of them over the past couple of months to know that they were endearing little devils. It wouldn't take much for them to make her go all mushy inside and then where would they all be when Duke packed his bags and took off for a new oil field? Sooner or later, he would. He hated being chained to a desk too much not to balk at it sooner or later.

"Forget it," she said succinctly.

"Then I guess you won't mind if I check him out," Jenny said.

Dani flinched at the suggestion but forced herself to shrug indifferently. "It's up to you. I have no claim on Duke Jenkins."

Jenny's stare was penetrating and disconcerting. "You're sure?" she persisted.

"I said so, didn't I?" she snapped testily.

"Okay, then. If we don't hook up again before I leave today, I'll see you tomorrow, right?"

Dani nodded and watched Jenny circle the pool in Duke's direction. Along the way she was waylaid by Sharon Lynn. Dani swore that the little whoosh of relief she felt had nothing at all to do with Jenny's failure to hook up with Duke. She didn't care who the man dated. He could go out with the entire female population of Los Pinos for all she cared, Jenny included. In fact, she was the one who'd first suggested they would make a good pair.

So why did the prospect still set off this odd little aching sensation in the region of her heart? she wondered. Lunacy, she concluded. Maybe exercise would restore the blood flow to her brain.

When everyone else headed for dinner on the patio, she remained in the pool. She swam laps, which had been impossible when it had been jammed. She was praying the exercise would wipe out the thoughts of the man who had been plaguing her for weeks now. She was running out of excuses to avoid him. She'd been so sure he would take the hint eventually, but he'd shown no signs of doing so. In fact, it appeared all she'd really succeeded in doing was increasing his fascination. He had an absolutely inspiring mix of patience and determination.

Jenny would probably take care of that, she thought irritably. She was a little surprised to hear that Jenny was interested in Duke, but she probably shouldn't have been. After all, he was a gorgeous, bright, funny man. What sane woman wouldn't be interested in him?

Breathless at last, she swam to the side of the pool and clung.

"Worn-out?" an amused voice inquired from above her. She looked up into sparkling blue eyes and felt that strange little sizzle Duke managed to set off without even trying.

"Pretty much," she confessed. "How come you're not eating dinner with everyone else?"

"It'll still be there in a few minutes."

"Don't count on it. Uncle Cody and Uncle Luke have very hearty appetites. And Harlan Patrick and Justin are virtually grown men. Everyone knows they can clean off a buffet table faster than a butler with a hand-vac."

He grinned. "You worried I'm going to starve? Or just anxious to be rid of me?"

"Why would I want to get rid of you?"

"Good question. Care to answer it?"

"If I've given you that impression, I'm sorry."

"Said very dutifully and very politely. Why don't I believe it?"

"Believe whatever you like."

"Let me hazard a guess instead," he suggested. "I think you're scared to be alone with me. Look at you now, for instance. You're shivering."

"The air's cold," she said defensively.

"It's ninety," he pointed out. "And the water's not that cold, either, in case you were thinking of mentioning that next."

"How would you know? You haven't been in."

He grinned. "Keeping an eye on me, were you?"

"You know I could really grow to dislike you," she muttered.

He didn't appear to be horrified by the prospect. "Really? I don't think so. I think exactly the opposite is true and it scares you silly."

"You really are full of yourself, aren't you?" she said as a mischievous idea popped into her head. "Maybe you should cool off."

Before he could guess what she intended, she snagged his arm and toppled him straight into the pool. If he hadn't been off balance to begin with she doubted she could have managed it, but he was. He came up sputtering with a look of astonishment on his face. She might have laughed, if she hadn't noted the calculating gleam in his eyes. He wanted revenge.

She pushed off from the wall and swam for the opposite end of the pool. She was fairly confident of her swimming skill, plus she had the element of surprise on her side. And Duke was weighed down with shorts, a T-shirt and sneakers. She should have made it. No question about it.

When she felt a hand wrap around her ankle, she yelped with surprise and took in a mouthful of water. Strong hands spanned her waist and lifted her up. Her legs instinctively circled Duke's waist and her hands came to rest on his shoulders. At least his skin wasn't bare, she thought as desire slammed through her. If it had been, if she'd felt that muscled flesh beneath her fingers, it would have been all over. Her pretense of being unaffected by him would have vanished like a puff of smoke caught by the wind.

As it was, she doubted he could mistake the pebbling of her nipples beneath the scanty fabric of her bathing suit. Nor could he miss the catch of her breath or the way her own flesh was suddenly burning. She was surprised steam wasn't rising all around them.

When she finally dared, she looked into his eyes and saw that he appeared to be almost as stunned as she was. Lust had darkened his eyes. Dani suspected she would find that same passionate hunger reflected in her own eyes. She had never, ever wanted a man as desperately as she did this one. Right here, right now. The powerful force of it stunned her.

Abstinence and avoidance, it appeared, had been a waste of time. It had had exactly the opposite effect of the one she'd hoped for. Caught up against his body, she was feverish with need.

"You picked a hell of a time for this," he murmured, his voice husky.

"For what?"

"To tempt me to make love to you."

"I am not..." she began, but the protest died on her lips when she saw he would never believe a denial. She managed a halfhearted smile. "You ought to be grateful, actually."

"Why is that?"

"Given the circumstances, we won't make a terrible mistake."

"Would it be so terrible?"

Unexpected tears formed in her eyes and spilled down her cheeks, mixing with chlorine. Hopefully, that would disguise them.

"You know it would be," she said.

"I don't know any such thing, darlin'."

Before they could debate the subject, a voice called out.

"Hey, Dani, you out here?" Justin shouted. "Dad says you'd better hurry or there won't be any barbecue left."

"I'll be there in a minute," she called back, thankful that they were in the shadowed end of the water, invisible in the gathering darkness.

"Want me to get you a towel?" her brother offered.

"No, thanks. Go on back. I'll be right there."

She heard a muttered exchange, then a chuckle.

"Tell Duke to hurry up, too," Harlan Patrick called out. "Before Uncle Jordan decides to see what's taking you so long."

Dani chuckled despite her embarrassment. "There are eyes and ears everywhere with this family."

"Should I expect Jordan to meet me with a shotgun in the morning?"

"You never know."

He winked at her. "I'll take my chances. It was worth it."

"How can you say that? Nothing happened," Dani said.

"Sure it did. I just got all the proof I need that my instincts were on track the first time I saw you."

Her gaze narrowed. "Meaning?"

"I'll explain it to you another time. I think we'd better join the others."

"Duke Jenkins, what did you mean?" she said, scurrying after his retreating back.

Naturally, since she was more intent on catching him than on where she was, she managed to snag his soaking wet shorts just as he stepped onto the patio, right smack in front of her grandfather.

"Everything okay?" Grandpa Harlan inquired, not even trying to hide his amusement.

"Just peachy," Dani said and allowed the elastic waistband to snap back into place.

Duke grinned. "Better than that, actually."

"Good," Grandpa Harlan said. "I couldn't be happier."

Oh, sweet heaven, what was the family going to make of this? Dani wondered desperately. Not that the answer was all that difficult to figure out. They were going to assume whatever they wanted to. She could talk a blue streak for an entire year, and they would never believe that nothing had happened between her and Duke. For some reason, that didn't seem to bother him one bit.

She whirled around and scowled at him. "This is all your fault, you know."

"What's my fault?" he asked innocently.

If he couldn't see the hornet's nest they'd stirred up, she wasn't going to explain it to him. Let him find out for himself when her father cornered him first thing in the morning. She grinned vindictively. What she wouldn't give to be a fly on the wall when Duke tried squirming off the hook that he'd inadvertently managed to snag himself on.

"Are you making any progress?" Jordan asked Duke at their regular weekly planning meeting, which had been rescheduled for eight a.m. Tuesday because of the holiday.

"On what?" Duke inquired, feigning ignorance. He had a hunch they were not talking business. Jordan had taken to lumping the strategy for his personal life into the same sessions at which they discussed acquisitions and mergers.

"With my daughter, of course."

"You were at the picnic yesterday. You know as much as I do."

Jordan sighed heavily. "The girl's as elusive as a will-o'-the-wisp, isn't she? Just like her mother."

"Kelly was hard to get?" Duke asked. "For some reason I thought you two were childhood sweethearts."

Jordan grinned. "Depends on whom you ask. She

claims she was always crazy about me, but I kept chasing after unsuitable women. When I finally woke up and decided the right woman had been under my nose all along, she turned me down. Again and again, in fact.''

Duke was astonished. He'd never read an article about his boss in any newspaper or magazine in which some mention hadn't been made of the enduring love of his life. It was hard to imagine that theirs hadn't always been a fairy-tale love story. He had envied them that. It was something he never expected to experience.

"Really?" he asked. "Why didn't she accept your proposal?"

"She claimed she was only waiting for me to admit I loved her and Dani. Personally, I think she was paying me back for all that trial and error with those other women.''

Duke found Jordan's revelations more disturbing than he dared to admit. If Kelly had held out for an admission of love from a man she openly adored, would her daughter ever accept less from a man? Duke couldn't offer her love. He didn't have it in him.

He could promise her loyalty and faithfulness, companionship and friendship. He could offer her a family. Would that be enough to entice her to marry him? Or would she tell him to go hire a nanny, if all he wanted was someone to look after his sons? Unfortunately, he could practically hear her saying just that. Shouting it, in fact, at the top of her lungs.

Of course, he did have one ace in the hole. The attraction between them was powerful enough to singe asbestos. Some women confused sexual attraction with love. Few men did. He certainly didn't. He just prayed that Dani was one of the women who would never sleep with a man she didn't fancy herself head over heels in love with. Then, once he'd made love to her, he would be halfway to getting her to marry him.

Of course, he still hadn't even succeeded in getting her to go on a damn date, but he would rectify that this afternoon at four at Dolan's. The rest would follow.

He hoped.

Chapter Eight

"Hey, sweetie," Sharon Lynn said, when Dani walked into Dolan's promptly at four on Tuesday. "Lemonade? Or are you going to splurge on a milk shake? You haven't had one in a while."

"Since Jenny's buying, I was thinking of a hot fudge sundae," Dani said, already imagining the taste of the thick, warm chocolate drenching the chilly, creamy vanilla. If she had any vices, this was it. It had been weeks since she'd last indulged herself. There were a hundred and one reasons she deserved that sundae. Putting up with—no, surviving—Duke Jenkins was at the top of the list.

Aware of Dani's recent restraint, Sharon Lynn grinned. "Sure thing," she said and began scooping vanilla ice cream into a deep, old-fashioned glass dish before Dani could have second thoughts.

Dani glanced around the deserted drugstore. "Where's Jenny? I thought she'd be here on the dot since she was so insistent on me being here at four."

"Oh, she probably got caught up in something out at White Pines," Sharon Lynn said without meeting her gaze. "You know how Grandpa Harlan is with his little projects. He loves having Jenny home so he can try to boss her around."

"Try being the operative word," Dani said, smiling. "No one ever succeeds in getting Jenny to do anything she doesn't want to do, Grandpa included."

"Much to his chagrin," Sharon Lynn added, handing her the sundae.

"She was a rebellious fourteen-year-old when he married Janet and adopted Jenny. You would think he'd have figured out by now that she's not going to change."

"Grandpa is the most optimistic man on earth. You know that," Sharon Lynn said. "Plus he managed to manipulate all but one of his stubborn sons into doing what he wanted. He's a master of reverse psychology. Why should he give up on Jenny?"

"That's not quite right," Dani countered soberly. "Even Uncle Erik followed Grandpa's wishes and became a rancher. We all know what a tragic mistake that was. He died because of it. You would have thought that would cure Grandpa of meddling."

Both she and Sharon Lynn fell silent. She had only very dim memories of Erik Adams. Sharon Lynn hadn't even been born when the accident on Uncle Luke's ranch had happened. Still, they both had heard of the heavy cost Grandpa Harlan had paid for pushing Erik into a career for which he wasn't at all suited. Maybe every member of the Adams clan was destined to make one huge mistake in a lifetime. Hopefully, Rob had been her one and only disaster.

Then again, maybe there was another terrible calamity on the horizon, she thought as she heard Duke's cheerful greeting to Sharon Lynn. The spoon almost slipped out of her suddenly shaky grasp when she felt his fingers skim her shoulder in a light caress as he slid onto the stool next to her. Yes, indeed, disaster was definitely right around the corner.

"Hey, darlin'. Fancy meeting you here," he said. "Sharon Lynn, how about a cup of coffee and a piece of lemon meringue pie?"

Dani slowly swiveled around until she could look directly into his eyes.

The glint she detected seemed an awful lot like triumph. Duke had never struck her as the kind of man who'd be tempted to play hooky in the middle of a workday. Nor was Dolan's so close to his office that he would be likely to pop in for take-out coffee, not when Jordan maintained a fully stocked snack bar for his employees and a dining room for executives.

Besides, Duke wasn't even dressed for work. He'd taken time to go home and change from a business suit into chinos and a T-shirt that emphasized the breadth of his chest and the muscles in his arms. She should be used to the fact that he was devastating no matter what he wore, but she wasn't.

Since he was very much here in the middle of a workday, there was only one conclusion she could reach. He had to be up to something and the something was related to her.

But how the heck would he have known...? One look at Sharon Lynn's expression answered that. Guilt was written all over her face. Dani turned back to Duke.

"Why aren't you at the office?" she inquired suspiciously.

The corners of his mouth tilted into the beginnings of a smile. "Is this an official inquiry or casual chit-chat?"

"Whichever will get me a straight answer."

"I'm all caught up on my work," he said as if he were a kid swearing that all his homework was done. "Jordan gave me permission to take the rest of the day off."

Dani regarded him skeptically. "You asked?"

"Of course. I always play by the rules."

"Oh, please," she protested. "You don't expect me to believe that one, do you?"

He grinned. "It was worth a shot," he said and took a bite of his pie.

"It failed. Now try the truth. Why are you here?"

He took his own sweet time about answering. First, he tried another bite of the pie Sharon Lynn had set down, then a couple of swallows of coffee. Dani was fighting exasperation by the time he met her gaze.

"Actually, someone mentioned that this would be a good time to catch up with Josh and Zack," he said turning a pointed look on Sharon Lynn, who was suddenly very busy counting out little piles of napkins on the far side of the U-shaped counter. "Have you seen them today?"

"No." Dani watched her cousin trying to slip unobtrusively into the storage room. No question Sharon Lynn was in this—whatever *this* was—up to her eyeballs.

"Are you expecting them?" Duke asked.

Dani's gaze narrowed. "Why would I be expecting them?" Suddenly the whole convoluted plot began to come clear. She stared at her cousin, who'd almost made it into the safety of that back room. "Sharon Lynn, get back here. What do you know about this?"

"About what?" her cousin asked defensively.

"Me being here? Duke turning up? What's the deal?"

"Deal? There's no deal," she insisted, not coming one step closer. "I have no idea what you're talking about."

"Why you little..." Duke began, then suddenly grinned. "You're good. You know that. You are really good."

Sharon Lynn blushed.

Dani stared from one to the other. "Would one of you tell me what's going on?"

Since Sharon Lynn's lips were clamped firmly shut, it was Duke who answered. "We've been had, darlin'. Set up. Manipulated. Meddled with."

That pretty much confirmed Dani's own suspicions. After all, Jenny was nowhere in sight, either. Their scheming left her momentarily speechless.

"Let me guess," Duke suggested. "You were lured here to meet...?"

"Jenny," she supplied with a sigh.

"Any sign of her?"

"No." She scowled at her cousin. "Sharon Lynn?"

"Yes?"

"What are you two up to?" she asked again, though by now the answer was fairly obvious.

Fortunately, for her cousin, the phone in the storage room rang.

"Sorry," Sharon Lynn said, not sounding the least bit sorry. She made a relieved dash out of sight.

"That's probably Jenny now," Duke speculated. "Checking to see how things are progressing."

When Sharon Lynn was gone, Dani regarded Duke apologetically. "I'm the one who's truly sorry. They shouldn't have put you in this position."

He grinned and popped the last bite of pie into his mouth. "The way I see it there's nothing wrong with the position I'm in. The pie was great. The coffee's the best in town. The company's not bad. What about you? Enjoying your sundae?"

Dani considered lying, but decided it was a waste of time and good hot fudge sauce. "Yes," she admitted.

"Then eat up." He leaned closer. "Then we'll sneak out without paying. That'll serve 'em right."

She grinned at his notion of revenge. "I don't think the cost of a hot fudge sundae and some pie and coffee is going to teach those two a lesson. For that matter, they can probably get Grandpa Harlan to ante up for it. I detect his fine hand in here somewhere. I can just see the three of them in his den out at White Pines plotting and scheming.''

''Maybe we should give them something to think about,'' Duke suggested, a worrisome glint back in his eyes.

''Such as?''

Even as she spoke, she realized she should never have asked. Those two words were as good as asking for trouble.

Duke swiveled her stool around until their knees were touching. His gaze locked with hers. Dani felt the sizzle of that look all the way down to her toes. If hot fudge was a vice, this was pure sin, she concluded.

She told herself she was going to look away any second now. She was going to move away from the graze of chinos against her knees and the lure of Duke's body heat. Any minute now, she promised herself.

Her breath caught in her throat. This was a dangerous game they were playing. In fact, they were flat-out flirting with disaster. If it could be called flirting, when the man looked as if he were one heartbeat away from scooping her up and hauling her off to bed, she amended. They were way beyond flirting.

When his callused fingertips skimmed along her cheek, her pulse zoomed straight into the stratosphere. When his thumb brushed over her lower lip, she felt the jolt in every cell from head to toe. She swallowed hard and willed herself to look away, move, get up and haul butt out of there.

Instead, she seemed to sway toward him, just when

his head was swooping in and his lips were taking dead-on aim for hers. The kiss, which she was so sure had been the last thing on her mind, turned out to be as inevitable as breathing. Soft and sweet and tender, it left her feeling cherished in a way that she'd never, ever felt before.

"Oh, boy," she whispered, when he had pulled away. She was in trouble, hip-deep and sinking fast.

"Nice," Duke assessed. "But I'm thinking that's not enough to convince them we don't need their help."

"Hmm?" she murmured, too dazed to follow his thinking. She blinked as he slowly rose to his feet, gasped softly when he lifted her until she was standing toe-to-toe with him, close enough that his heat surrounded her, beckoned to her.

His fingers tunneled through her hair. His breath whispered against her cheek. And then his mouth covered hers again.

This time there was nothing soft or sweet or tender about the kiss. It was demanding and hungry and possessive. And it took her breath away. It dazzled her. In fact, in her personal range of experience, this was the mother of all kisses, the kind that could lure a woman into thinking she was in love.

That four-letter word slipped into her consciousness even as Duke deepened the kiss to a whole new level of bone-melting bliss. Love. *LOVE?* Whoa, baby.

Dani felt the emotional brakes slam on. She spun away from Duke so quickly she left both of them off balance and shaky. Clearly surprised, he regarded her intently.

"Dani, talk to me."

Embarrassment flooded over her. She had practically come apart in Duke's arms right in the middle of a public place. It was the kind of behavior that started rumors and caused pain. All they needed was for Joshua and Zachary to get wind of the incident. They were clearly eager for a new mom. One whiff of this and those fertile eight-year-old minds would start manufacturing all sorts of happily-ever-after scenarios that just weren't going to happen. She forced herself to look directly into Duke's eyes.

"This is never going to happen again," she said bluntly. "Never."

Apparently, her tone was more convincing than usual because for once he didn't argue, didn't make some teasing remark or offer up a challenge that would have turned her vow into a joke. In fact, he nodded solemnly as if he'd gotten the message loud and clear.

"Never," he echoed.

"Promise me," she said, just to be sure.

"This will never happen again, I swear it," he said.

He sounded sincere enough, she supposed, but for some reason she trusted him about as much as she trusted Sharon Lynn and Jenny at the moment. She glanced at his hands, checking for crossed fingers. If she could have she would have checked his toes as well. Nope, there were no overt signs that he was intentionally lying through his teeth.

"I'm taking you at your word," she said. "My

father says you're an honorable man. I'm counting on it.''

That seemed to make him uneasy, but again he nodded dutifully. ''You can count on it, darlin'.''

He said it so easily that she was vaguely insulted. Didn't he want to kiss her again? Had it been awful for him? What the heck was the matter with him that he was giving up so easily?

No, what was the matter with her that she wasn't taking his promise at face value and hightailing it back to the safety of the clinic? Hormones evidently played havoc with logic.

She stiffened her spine, picked up her purse and inched away from Duke, careful not to brush against him. She was being absurd. It wasn't as if the man was going to grab her and throw her on the counter and have his way with her. He'd just promised he wouldn't even kiss her again, for heaven's sakes.

Of course, there was no guarantee that she wouldn't be the one doing the throwing and the having. Maybe that was why it was very wise not to come within a mile of Duke Jenkins for at least the next forty or fifty years. Maybe by then her hormones would be in check. If they weren't, it would probably be some sort of medical miracle and they could go on TV on some X-rated sex channel for seniors. The thought of it made her smile.

''Dani?''

She blinked and met his gaze, fully aware that color was flooding her cheeks again. She had blushed more in the past few weeks than she had in her entire life before meeting Duke. ''Yes?''

"Want me to walk you back to your clinic?"

"No," she blurted at once, then winced at the rude tone. "I mean, really it's not necessary."

He regarded her doubtfully. "You seem a little wobbly."

"I am not," she said emphatically. "Once I'm out in the fresh air, I'll be just fine."

"It's a hundred degrees out there."

So what? she thought. It had to be darned close to that inside when they were in the middle of that kiss. In fact, she probably ought to speak to Sharon Lynn about fixing the thermostat on the air conditioner. It was way too hot in Dolan's. In fact, she was tempted to pick up a menu and fan herself right now, but she could see how Duke might misconstrue that and turn it into some sort of admission that he affected her.

"The heat doesn't bother me," she insisted, backing away an inch at a time as if she were trying to slip away without him noticing.

"If you say so."

"I do."

"Then I guess I'll see you around."

"Right."

"Bye."

"Bye."

"Have a pleasant evening."

"You, too." Dani sighed. Much more of this polite leave-taking and she was going to throw up. Before she added that to the list of her most embarrassing moments, she bolted for the door.

The blast of humid heat should have slowed her down. She barely even noticed it as she practically ran all the way back to the clinic. She headed straight for her own part of the house. She'd left the air conditioning set at a pleasant seventy-five degrees. She turned it down to sixty and went and stood in front of a register and let the cool air blow over her.

Even when her body was shivering and the cats were trying to crawl under an afghan on the sofa, she still felt hot. Only then did she admit to herself that as long as Duke remained at the center of her thoughts it wouldn't matter if she bathed in ice water. She'd still be burning up.

Duke didn't glance away from the door through which Dani had exited until he heard a whisper of sound behind him. He turned to find Sharon Lynn regarding him warily. After a moment, she bravely forced a smile.

"More coffee?" she inquired cheerfully.

"I think maybe I'd better switch to iced tea," he said. "With lots and lots of ice."

"I noticed it got pretty warm in here," she said.

"I'm delighted we were able to provide the entertainment. Now maybe you can tell me something."

"What?"

"Exactly what were you and Jenny up to? It's fairly obvious to me that Dani does not want a new man in her life, especially not one who's a single father, right?"

"That's what she thinks."

Duke's gaze narrowed. "Am I missing something? Isn't what she thinks important?"

"Not if it's different from what she feels," Sharon

Lynn explained patiently. "This afternoon proves what we suspected all along. She's attracted to you. She's just scared to death of doing anything about it. That's understandable, of course. But you can't stop living just because you've been burned by an idiot, right?"

"I suppose."

"Let me ask you something. Are you interested in Dani? I mean beyond a quick roll in the hay or something?"

"Isn't that an awfully personal question?"

Sharon Lynn shrugged off the implied criticism. "I'm an Adams," she said as if that were explanation enough. "We're nosy, especially when it comes to one of our own. Now stop avoiding the question. Are your intentions serious?"

Duke shook his head, amused by the persistence, if not by the prying. "I think Dani's the only one who deserves an answer to that question and she's not asking it."

"She won't, either. It's up to the rest of us to protect her."

"Would she appreciate you doing that?"

"Of course not," Sharon Lynn conceded airily. "But she'd expect it just the same. When it comes to providing backup, we're better than the Texas Rangers."

"I see. Well, let me give you just a little bit of advice from an outsider's perspective. The game is underway. Stay on the sidelines from here on out and watch. I think Dani and I can take it from here."

Sharon Lynn grinned. "Yes, I imagine you can do just about anything you set your mind to."

"I'll take that as a compliment."

"Of course you will," she said. "And I will stay out of it, unless I think you're getting out of line. Then I can pretty much guarantee someone in the family will call the foul."

He regarded her with amusement. "And the penalty?"

She returned his look solemnly. "You don't want to know."

Duke shook his head. "Your uncle Jordan said practically the same thing."

She grinned. "As long as you've gotten the message."

"Loud and clear, sweetheart. Loud and clear."

But the only signals he was really worried about were the ones Dani was sending him and those were very, very mixed.

Chapter Nine

Duke was constantly revising his strategy where Dani was concerned. After that last kiss, he concluded that she needed time to think about it, lots of time. He made himself so scarce that the only people who saw him regularly were his sons, Paolina, Jordan and his secretary. September eased into October, then November. Let Dani start to wonder what he was up to. Maybe it would force her to admit she was intrigued by him.

At least that was his theory. In practice, he was the one going stark-raving nuts. The boys weren't doing especially well with the forced confinement, either. They'd been plaguing him daily about going out to White Pines to see the horses or into town for ice cream. They were getting to be almost as restless and cranky as he was. He might not be experienced at this parenting business, but he sensed that something was going to have to give very soon.

Sitting in his study, he tried to focus on the paperwork he'd brought home from the office, but his mind wasn't on it. He was downright ecstatic when Joshua came to stand in the doorway, regarding him solemnly.

"Hey, son, what's up?"

"Are you busy?"

"Not too busy for you. Come on in."

Joshua bounded across the room and to Duke's astonishment climbed into his lap and burrowed his face against Duke's chest. His narrow little shoulders heaved with barely contained sobs. Duke had never felt so helpless in his entire life. He wrapped the boy in his arms and held on tight.

"Josh, what's going on?" he asked eventually, when the crying had abated somewhat.

"Nothing," Joshua replied, sniffing.

Duke smiled, grateful that Josh couldn't see it. "That's an awful lot of tears over nothing. Did something happen at school today?"

"No."

"What then?"

Joshua pulled back and looked straight into Duke's eyes. His little face was streaked with tears. "Dad, how come Mommy doesn't love us?"

Oh, boy, Duke thought, biting back a sigh. "What makes you think she doesn't love you? We've talked about this before, remember? It's me she's mad at, not you guys."

"I don't think so. I think she hates all of us. Me and Zack, too."

Duke began to get a sneaking suspicion about the cause of the tears. "Did she call here today?"

Josh hesitated, then sniffed and nodded. "She told us not to tell you, Dad, I didn't mean to break the promise, honest."

"That's okay. Some promises should never be made in the first place. You should always be able to come to me. If someone tells you not to, always ask yourself why. Now tell me what your mom said that upset you so much."

"Zack and me asked her to come home. We told her we missed her a whole lot, but she said no." Fresh tears welled up in his eyes. "She said she was never, ever coming back."

Duke mentally cursed Caroline for being so blunt with the two boys, then swearing them to secrecy. Did she expect them to keep all the hurt bottled up inside? Or were the secrets just meant as payback for him?

He wiped away Josh's tears and tried to coax a smile from him. "Now you listen to me, half-pint. We're getting along okay, just the three of us, right?"

"Yeah, but it would be nice to have a mom again," Josh said wistfully.

Duke immediately thought of Dani. She might not be able to replace Caroline in their hearts, but she could fill an obvious void in their lives. It was time to move on to the next step in his strategy. If nothing else, this conversation with Josh had proven that it was time to start courting Dani in earnest.

* * *

Duke had given Dani so much space she was about to spit. Not even reminding herself a hundred times a day that she had asked for it seemed to help. Work took up most of her time, but there were always a few hours late at night when she had nothing to do but think and remember the way she had felt in Duke's arms smack in the middle of Dolan's.

That kiss was the most impulsive, uninhibited thing she'd ever done. Naturally, she couldn't get it out of her head, she consoled herself. It had nothing to do with Duke *per se*. It was the outrageous risk she'd taken that was plaguing her.

So why did she glance hopefully at the door to her office every time it opened unexpectedly? Why did she spend a solid hour primping before every single family gathering on the chance that Duke would be invited? Why was she so disappointed when he never turned up?

Perversity was one possibility. Insanity was another. Admitting that she was falling in love with the man despite her best intentions was not an acceptable explanation. A few breath-stealing kisses didn't amount to a hill of beans in the overall scheme of life. She would forget all about them soon enough. She just had to concentrate on other things.

"Such as?" she muttered testily to herself.

"Such as what?"

The masculine voice, which surely she had conjured up, sent a shiver dancing down her spine. Obviously, the attraction hadn't worn off, she thought glumly as she glanced up at the man filling the doorway to her office. He was back in a business suit and more devastatingly handsome than ever. Just the sound of his deep, husky voice was enough to make her pulse skitter crazily. If anyone took an EKG right now, it would land her in the hospital. She forced herself not to drag in a deep breath, sigh, swallow or otherwise indicate that he'd rattled her by popping up when she least expected him.

"Just talking to myself," she said, pleased with her calm, casual tone. "What brings you by?"

"An emergency. Well, two emergencies, actually."

Her professional mode kicked in. She was on her feet and halfway around her desk, when he put out a hand to stop her.

"Whoa! I didn't mean medical emergencies. Sorry."

She frowned at him. "It's not a word we take lightly around here."

"I know. I should have realized that."

"There are no half-drowned kittens, then?"

He grinned. "Nothing like that. The cats have gotten very adept at avoiding Joshua and Zachary. They seem to have a sixth sense when the two of them are up to no good."

"That's the beauty of cats," Dani agreed. "They're pretty good at fending for themselves."

"Like you," he suggested lightly.

She wasn't entirely sure if he meant it as an insult or a compliment. "I suppose," she agreed. She regarded him expectantly.

"Actually, I've been meaning to call," he began, but Dani cut him off.

"You don't need to explain. We agreed that we wouldn't see each other again."

He seemed surprised by the statement. "Is that what we agreed?"

There was that worrisome gleam in his eyes again. "Of course, it is," she said hurriedly. "I told you—"

"Specifically that I was never to kiss you in the middle of Dolan's again."

Dani's gaze narrowed. She thought she detected an opening there for other kisses in other places, when nothing could have been further from her intentions. Explaining that, though, might be considered an over-reaction since he'd shown no particular inclination even to see her again lately.

"More or less," she said. She decided there was probably safer conversational turf for them to be on, especially since Duke seemed to be staring at her as if he hadn't been near a woman in a hundred years and desperation was setting in. Since her own level of yearning had reached a fever pitch, they were heading for trouble unless one of them changed the topic to something a little less sexual.

"You still haven't explained about the so-called emergency," she said hurriedly.

He blinked at the reminder. "Yeah, right."

"Well?"

He glanced around her office. "Do you think maybe we could have this conversation someplace else?"

"Why?"

He regarded her with amusement. "Because I

asked nicely?'' he suggested. "We could go out for pizza. That wouldn't be too dangerous, would it?''

Dani winced at the suggestion that she found being alone with him dangerous. She had hoped he would interpret their last parting as a lack of interest on her side. Obviously, he'd reached just the opposite conclusion.

"Duke, please…''

"It's not a date,'' he assured her. "It's just that I'm starved. It's around dinnertime. Why not have it together so we can discuss things.''

"Things?'' she repeated. "What things?''

He grinned. "I'll explain over pizza.''

"Duke!''

"Please.''

She could turn him down. She could manufacture other plans, but the honest to goodness truth was, she didn't want to. One sight of him standing in the doorway to her office and she'd reacted to his presence the way a parched man would to an oasis. Just because she didn't want to get involved with him didn't mean they couldn't be friends, did it? Perhaps that was all he was offering, she told herself, though the unmistakable heat in his eyes said otherwise.

"It will have to be a quick dinner,'' she said. "I need to drive out to Betty Lou's and take a look at Honeybunch.''

Duke stared at her with obvious surprise. "I thought he'd be fully recovered by now.''

"Actually, he is, but Betty Lou is lonely. She got used to me dropping in when I first took Honeybunch home.''

Duke grinned. "The truth is, you miss that dog, don't you?"

"Well, he was around the clinic for several weeks," she said defensively. "Besides, it's more than that. Betty Lou has some terrific stories about Grandpa Harlan when he was a boy. I'm recording them all so I can blackmail him if the need ever arises."

"Now that does sound like a reason to keep calling," Duke agreed. "Mind if I tag along? We can drive out there first, then eat."

"I thought you were starving."

"I won't die from it."

"Okay, if you're sure. I'm warning you, though. Betty Lou is liable to make a pass at you. She considers herself to be quite a femme fatale."

Duke returned her teasing gaze evenly. "I can hardly wait. I've been worried I was losing my touch."

They found Betty Lou fixing fried chicken and mashed potatoes, enough for an army. She invited them in without any evidence at all that she was surprised by their arrival.

"Betty Lou, this is Duke Jenkins," Dani said.

Betty Lou batted long, thick, mascaraed eyelashes at the man in question. "Oh, honey, I know who this is. Not a woman in town hasn't been speculating why a handsome catch like this is still on the loose." She looked Duke over from head to toe, then gave a little nod of approval. "How do you feel about older women?"

To his credit, he managed to keep a straight face.

"I'd say that depends. If they're as beautiful as you, I'd say my mind is open."

"Then sit right down here. Dani, you, too," she added as an afterthought. "You're staying for dinner."

"But we intended to go out for pizza," Dani protested.

Betty Lou waved the long fork she was holding in a dismissive gesture. "You can have pizza any old time. I've got mashed potatoes, corn and a peach pie to go with this chicken. Now tell me you can turn down home-cooking like that."

"Not me," Duke said, eyeing the pots on the stove avidly. When his gaze reached the huge peach pie with the golden crust, he practically salivated.

Dani decided to save her breath. She would just have to wait until after dinner to discover what had been on Duke's mind when he turned up in her office. Besides, they were probably better off with a chaperone, especially one who had her own designs on Duke.

"Dinner sounds lovely," she agreed. "Where's Honeybunch, by the way?"

"Out chasing squirrels last time I checked. He'll be dragging back here any second looking for something to eat."

"He's doing okay?"

"Better than okay," Betty Lou said. "He's taking full advantage of that new lease on life you gave him. I don't know how to thank you."

"You've already thanked me," Dani said. "A hundred times, in fact."

"Maybe so, but I know you would have put any other dog in that condition to sleep," Betty Lou said. "Maybe I should have, too, but I just couldn't bear it. He's been my companion for too long now. I expected to go to my grave long before he did. You can bet I gave that drunk driver a piece of my mind when I caught up with him down at the jail. It was bad enough that he hit the dog to begin with, but to just leave him in the road like that was a real heartless crime."

"The judge sentenced him to volunteer in a hospital emergency room for six months once he gets out of jail," Dani said. "The judge told him he wants him to get a good, up-close look at the victims of traffic accidents before he gets behind the wheel again."

Betty Lou shrugged off the justice. "The man's trash," she said. "He won't get the message. He'll end up dead sooner or later, which wouldn't bother me a bit, if it weren't for the guarantee that he'll be taking some innocent soul out with him." She shook her head. "Enough of this. You two didn't come all the way out here to listen to me go on and on."

"Actually, in a way we did," Duke told her. "Dani said you have some great stories about her grandfather."

"Harlan?" Betty Lou said with a chuckle. "That old coot and I go way back. Not that he likes to admit it. Ever since he married that young attorney, he pretends he's shaved a couple of decades off his age. Let me get all this food on the table and I'll tell you a thing or two about Harlan Adams."

For the next hour she regaled them with stories from her own school days. Grandpa Harlan seemed to play a pivotal role in most of them.

"Did you, by any chance, have a crush on my grandfather?" Dani teased.

"Heavens, no. Now that brother of his…"

Dani stared at her. "Brother? Grandpa Harlan had a brother?"

"Well, of course, he did. Henry Adams. Everyone around here called him Hank. Now there was a looker."

Dani was stunned. She had never once heard anyone in the family mention that name. "Did he die or something?"

"Not as far as I know," Betty Lou said. "There was some kind of falling out. He left town when he was quite young, maybe sixteen. He was quite a few years younger than your grandfather. He just took off. As far as I know, no one's heard from him since."

"Well, I'll be," Dani murmured.

A half hour later with the dishes done and Betty Lou openly yawning, Dani and Duke made their excuses and left. When they had climbed into his car, he glanced over at her. "I gather you've never heard of this great-uncle Hank."

"Never. Apparently Grandpa Harlan is even better at keeping secrets than he is at prying into them."

Duke considered that, his expression thoughtful. "Maybe you should leave well enough alone," he said. "If he hasn't mentioned his brother in all these years, it must have been a bitter feud. It might really upset him to bring it up at this late date."

"I suppose," she said disappointed, but unable to argue with his logic. She would ask her father about Hank Adams, though. Maybe he or Luke knew something about the man.

At the moment, though, there was another secret she needed to get to the bottom of. "When are you going to tell me what brought you to my office this afternoon?" she asked.

"Invite me in for coffee when we get to your place," he countered. "This isn't something we can discuss in the car."

"Why?"

"Because I need to get a clear look at your face when I bring it up."

She stared back at him nervously. "Uh-oh. I don't like the sound of that."

He grinned. "It's nothing to fret over, darlin'. You'll either say yes—" his gaze settled on her mouth "—or no."

Dani's heart thumped unsteadily for the second time that day. Yes or no? People said yes or no to proposals. Marriage proposals. Surely, if he'd gotten the message about kissing, then he would understand that it stood to reason she wouldn't be interested in marriage, right? Or had he just capitulated easily on the kissing, knowing that he had a bigger goal in mind?

Oh, for heaven's sakes, stop, she told herself sharply. This wasn't about marriage. It was about...well, who knew what it was about, she concluded, eyeing Duke warily. Anything was possible, especially with a man as unpredictable as Duke. She would probably laugh herself silly when she realized how far off the mark she'd been.

At the moment, though, trepidation was tearing through her at an astonishing clip. If she could have thought of any rational excuse, she would have bolted from the car in a flash. Heck, she would have packed her bags and moved out of Los Pinos to avoid having this conversation.

As it was, Duke was pulling into her driveway, cutting the engine and turning to her expectantly, obviously awaiting the invitation in for coffee. Dani swallowed hard and mumbled the invitation without much enthusiasm.

Duke regarded her with amusement. "Darlin', lighten up. This isn't about walking hand in hand to the gallows."

"Yeah, go tell that to someone who'll buy it," she muttered under her breath even as she led the way inside.

She flipped on every single light in the house as she passed through on her way to the kitchen. Forget cozy and romantic. She wanted illumination. She wanted it so bright, he would never mistake the ambience for an invitation. In fact, it wouldn't be bad if the lighting brought to mind a police interrogation room. Not that she'd ever been in one personally, but maybe Duke had.

She put the coffee on to brew, found a couple of old mugs so he would understand that this wasn't a special occasion, poured some fresh sugar in the sugar bowl even though it was already half-full and put milk into a cream pitcher, despite the fact that they both drank their coffee black. When there was absolutely nothing else left to do, she finally sat down opposite him.

"Finished?" he inquired, not bothering to hide a smile.

She scowled, annoyed by his amusement. "Yes."

"Are you sure you don't want to dash off and check the mail or dust the living room?"

"Duke, will you just spit out whatever's on your mind and go? I have a splitting headache, and I have an early day tomorrow."

He was on his feet in a flash and moving behind her. She twisted to see what he was up to, but he rested his hands on her shoulders until she sighed and faced forward again.

"Duke! What do you think you're doing?"

"You said you have a headache," he explained patiently as he began to massage her temples.

Dani would have protested, but it felt too good. She could feel the tension beginning to ease even before his fingers began kneading the hard knots in her shoulders.

"No wonder your head's pounding," he observed. "You're tense."

"Well, of course, I'm tense. You've been dropping little hints all evening that you have something important to discuss. My imagination is running wild."

"Really? I'm fascinated. Just what sort of images have you managed to conjure up?"

"Never mind."

He chuckled. "Whoops, here come those knots

again. They'd probably go away if you'd tell me what you've been thinking.''

"They would go away if you would just say what's on your mind and get out of here,'' she countered.

"Tsk, tsk, that's not a very auspicious beginning,'' he taunted. "Maybe I'd better get into this another time, when you're not so cranky.''

"Get into what, dammit? And I am not cranky.''

He chuckled. "Yes, indeed, another time would be best. It'll keep.''

Before she knew what he intended, he leaned down, brushed a brotherly peck across her cheek and headed for the door.

"Duke!''

"Night, darlin'. It's been fun.''

"Duke Jenkins, if you walk out that door without explaining yourself, don't come back.''

The threat was wasted. He was already halfway to the car by the time she finished. Since he gave her a jaunty wave as he pulled out of the driveway, she could only assume he wasn't feeling the least bit threatened.

"Well, damn,'' she muttered, staring after him.

As he drove home, Duke whistled cheerfully and congratulated himself on an evening well spent. He'd proved to himself once again that Dani wasn't nearly as immune to him as she wanted to be.

He could guess precisely which path her imagination had led her down. In fact, he had deliberately chosen his words just to point her in the right direction. Yes and no were answers to a whole lot of questions, most of them innocuous enough. But spoken with a little hint of seductiveness, they clearly hinted at very provocative queries to come.

After planting that particular seed in her mind, he'd been somewhat surprised that she'd allowed him in the house at all, given her avowed aversion to any kind of future with another single dad.

He had also been careful the past few weeks to stay away from White Pines or any other place where she was likely to be. Since any invitation always included Joshua and Zachary, he'd turned them all down. He'd wanted Dani wondering what he was up to, not remembering that he had two sons underfoot.

In the long run, he figured his strategy would pay off. In the short run, he was very close to losing his mind. How had he missed the fact that rearing two boys could be so incredibly challenging? Maybe not as challenging as exploring for oil, but a darned close second.

Maybe it was because they were twins, but Josh and Zack seemed to think as a single unit, conspiring to get into the most amazing amount of mischief just when he thought he had everything under control. Thankfully, they hadn't scared off Paolina, but he knew with every fiber of his being that the housekeeper was no substitute for a real mom. He intended to give them one or die trying.

It would have been a heck of a lot simpler, of course, if he'd picked one who was a little more amenable to the idea. Then again, courting Dani Adams was just about fascinating enough to take his mind off the tedium of all that paperwork her daddy piled on his desk.

Chapter Ten

After a restless night Dani stepped outside at mid-morning on Saturday to get the paper and discovered two little boys sitting on the front steps. She stared at Josh and Zack, then automatically looked around for some sign of their father.

"Dad's not with us," Josh said as if he, like his father, was capable of reading her mind.

"So I see. How did you get here?"

"Paolina brought us," Zack said.

Dani fought the panicky feeling that had been automatic from the moment she met these two wonderful, emotionally scary kids. "She just left you on my doorstep?"

"We came to buy cat food," Zack said. "Paolina said she'd get it at the grocery store, but the cats like the kind you have better."

Dani nodded as if the explanation made perfect sense, which it obviously did to them. "Well, then, I guess you'd better come in and choose the flavors you want."

"Anything but liver," Josh told her. "That smells yucky."

"Not to a cat," Dani pointed out.

Both boys looked startled.

"I guess you're right," Josh said. "And it's their dinner."

Dani grinned at him. "Exactly." She led the way into her pet supply room and pointed to the rows of gourmet cat food in cans and bags. "Can you two pick what you want on your own?" she inquired hopefully.

Zack gave her a shy look and, to her astonishment, slipped his hand into hers. "No, we want you to help. Okay?"

The warmth of that little hand tucked trustingly into her own brought on a flood of bittersweet memories. Every bit of instinct for self-preservation protested that she should make up a plausible excuse, walk away and leave the two boys to their shopping. One look into two pairs of hopeful eyes told her she couldn't do it.

"I'll help," she said grimly.

The process of choosing took far longer than it should have. They claimed they wanted to learn about every single ingredient in every single brand she carried. She distrusted their enthusiasm, but their sweet little expressions were so innocent she chided herself for being overly suspicious.

When they had filled a shopping bag with their selections and had added toys for each cat, they stood back and admired their purchases.

"I think you two have made excellent choices," she told them. "You've picked a good variety of very healthy cat food. Did you want me to send the bill to your dad?"

The two exchanged guilty looks.

"That's okay," Josh said. "We'll pay for it. I mean, not right this second, but soon."

Dani's suspicions stirred again. "Is this coming out of your allowances?"

"Heck, no," Zack said. "Dad's coming to get us when he gets finished at the office. He'll pay you."

Dani stared at them in astonishment. "Your father is coming here?"

Two heads bobbed.

"When?"

"After he gets done at work."

"Did he happen to mention when that would be?"

"Before lunchtime, I guess. He said we could all go out to eat together."

Why that sneaky, low-down, devious snake. Obviously, Duke had plotted to leave the boys with her for an entire morning. How could he? What if she'd been called away on an emergency? What if she'd simply been too busy to look after them? She regarded the two boys, who were waiting quietly for her response, and sighed. There was no emergency, and she wasn't too busy.

"Why don't we take the shopping bag into the kitchen, and I'll make us all some hot chocolate."

"All right!" Josh said.

"And cookies?" Zack asked, only to be shushed by his brother with a warning that he wasn't being polite.

"You're s'pposed to wait till you're invited," Josh said.

"That's okay," Dani told them. "Actually, I was just thinking about baking some cookies."

"Really?" Zack asked. "Chocolate chip?"

"Zack!" Josh protested.

Dani chuckled. "It's okay. Chocolate chip are my favorite, too. I always keep a package of the slice-and-bake kind in the refrigerator."

"We know how to do those kind," Zack said proudly. "Paolina lets us."

"Good, then you can help me," Dani said, taking the package out and searching for a cookie sheet and a knife that would do the job without being too dangerous for clumsy little hands.

The morning passed in a blur of hot chocolate, cookies, laughter and talk of dinosaurs and spaceships. She hadn't had so much fun since...

No, she told herself sternly. She wasn't going to go there. Not today. Today she was simply going to enjoy the fact that two little boys with incredible imaginations and their daddy's charm were sharing their lives with her.

Later she would try very hard not to let her heart break.

Duke surveyed the scene in Dani's kitchen and smiled. His little plot was working out very nicely.

Left to their own devices, he'd known that Josh and Zack could climb over any wall Dani tried to erect between them.

He'd given Paolina very explicit instructions to make sure that everything went off without a hitch. She was to leave the boys at Dani's, then drive by twice over the next half hour to make sure they were inside. She had called him at the office to report that everything was *muy bueno,* very good.

Now that he had Dani guessing about his intentions, Duke had concluded that it was time to switch tactics once again. He intended to pester her like ants at a picnic. She'd been so sure she was in charge, that he'd accepted her terms for their relationship. He wanted to make certain she realized now that she'd been mistaken.

Today's unscheduled visit from Josh and Zack was just the start.

"Having fun?" he inquired as he knocked on the screen door and entered the kitchen.

Dani had a streak of chocolate on her cheek, marshmallow on her lips and fire flashing in her eyes. Her laughter faded at the sight of him.

"You and I need to talk," she said quietly. "Boys, can you put the rest of the cookies in the cookie jar for me?"

"Sure," they said at once, far more eagerly than they'd ever responded to one of Duke's directives.

As soon as she saw that they were doing as she'd asked, she walked into the living room. Duke followed, preparing himself for the barrage of questions he knew was coming.

"What on earth were you thinking?" she demanded the instant they were out of earshot of the boys.

"Excuse me?"

"I am not your baby-sitter."

"Of course not."

"I could have been out on a call."

"That was a possibility," Duke agreed. "Paolina was supposed to check to make sure you were here."

"I never spoke to Paolina. I found your sons sitting on my doorstep, looking for all the world as if they'd been abandoned there."

"Naturally, you took them in."

"Well, of course I did. What was I supposed to do?"

"You could have called me to come and get them," he said mildly.

Dani stared at him silently, then some of the fight seemed to drain out of her. "Yes, you're right. I suppose I could have done that."

"Any idea why you didn't? I mean especially if having them here was a bother."

"It wasn't a bother, not like you mean."

He nodded at that. "Good. I'm glad."

"They're terrific boys. You know that."

"I think so." He shrugged. "Well, if that's all, I guess we'll be on our way. I promised to take them to lunch."

She actually grinned sheepishly at that. "I doubt they're all that hungry. We've eaten a lot of cookies. It probably spoiled their appetite."

"I don't suppose missing lunch will kill them." He

paused and deliberately brushed a brotherly kiss across her cheek. "Thanks, again. How much do I owe you for the cat food?"

She stared at him, clearly flustered. Finally, she distractedly named an amount and accepted the cash. When he walked out the door, the boys in tow, she still looked as if she wasn't quite certain what had happened. Duke grinned all the way home.

Over the next few weeks he could see that the new approach was working better and better. Dani brightened perceptibly at the sight of him, then turned right around and pretended she couldn't stand to be near him. He knew it was pretense, because he made a point of using any legitimate excuse at all to touch her.

A quick kiss of a greeting, a seemingly inadvertent brushing of their knees when they were cleverly and deliberately seated next to each other at the Adams gatherings he'd started attending again, a lightning-fast caress of her cheek as he said good-night. She trembled visibly at each fleeting contact. Color bloomed in her cheeks. Exasperation and yearning warred in her eyes.

Of course, the game was taking its toll on him as well. Some nights he went home so aroused, it took a jog around the house and an icy shower before he could settle down and have any hope at all of getting to sleep. When he realized he was tempted to start warming a pan of milk at bedtime, he knew he was in serious trouble.

Yes, indeed, the more Duke saw of Dani Adams, the more intrigued he was. He hated that no matter what he tried, she continued to look a little aloof, a little sad. In the midst of the wildest, noisiest family celebration, she kept mostly to herself. Not even Sharon Lynn's or Jenny's best efforts could penetrate her shell for long.

After the cookie-baking episode, she was more careful than ever, it seemed, to avoid spending any time whatsoever with his sons, so careful that it was clear she desperately wanted to gather them into her arms for hugs. Only a fool wouldn't recognize that she was a woman just made for mothering. It was in her eyes as she watched them, a longing so deep, so fierce that it reaffirmed Duke's determination to make her their mother.

The boys sensed those maternal instincts, too. They gravitated to her at every Adams family event and though she was as skittish as a horse around a rattler, sooner or later she came around. Every single time.

Josh and Zack made her smile when no one else could. The smiles were cautious, tentative, to be sure, but they lifted Duke's spirits as much as any oil strike he'd ever made.

Dani seemed to be the only one who didn't get how much her warmth was valued. On some level, she clearly blamed herself for getting too caught up in the lives of those girls she'd ultimately lost. She thought she was the one who'd hurt them, when the truth was it was their father's cavalier attitude that had set them all up for anguish.

Duke would never make that mistake. He was a decisive man, always had been. Once he made a commitment, he stuck to it, for better or worse. He would have stayed married to Caroline, enduring the cold emptiness of the relationship if that had been what she wanted. Duty and honor were that important to him.

Now he wanted Dani Adams to become a significant part of Josh's and Zack's lives, a permanent part. The boys needed a mother's love. They needed Dani. And he would do whatever was necessary to get her for them. He owed it to them after the mess he'd made of his marriage to their mother. It was as simple and clear-cut as that for him.

His own feelings toward her were more complex. He enjoyed Dani's company. He wanted her in his bed. He had vowed to himself that he would always treat her the way she deserved to be treated. The only thing he couldn't promise her was love. He hoped that the things he could offer would be enough for a woman who understood the meaning and importance of family.

Thanksgiving was coming and he decided the holidays were the perfect time to step up his campaign, turn up the heat another notch, so to speak. Christmas would be the ideal, most romantic time to announce an engagement. He made that his goal and set up a strategic plan that corporate executives—Jordan included, he thought with a grim smile—would have envied.

Her family, bless them, cooperated by issuing an invitation for Thanksgiving dinner at White Pines. The message had been relayed by Jordan just that afternoon. Duke mentioned it to the boys when he got home that night, certain of their response.

"So, what do you think?" he asked.

"Cool," Joshua said. "Will there be turkey and dressing and pumpkin pie?"

"I imagine so," Duke said. He was fairly confident that this family would celebrate with old-fashioned excess when it came to their Thanksgiving feast.

"Will Dani be there?" Zachary asked.

"Of course."

"Are you gonna kiss her again?" Zack asked, proving that he was as adept as any Adams at sneaking up on people.

Duke held back a grin. "Maybe."

"Does that mean you and Dani are gonna get married?" Joshua asked. "I haven't got all this grown-up stuff figured out yet."

"Kissing sometimes leads to marriage," Duke conceded carefully.

"But what about you and Dani?" Josh persisted. "Are you guys gonna get married?"

Duke knew better than to set them up for disappointment. His plans were a little too iffy to make a firm declaration on the subject just yet, especially when anything he said was likely to be repeated. He could just imagine Dani's reaction to hearing the news of their impending wedding from someone else.

"We'll see," he equivocated.

More than once after a frustrating day behind his desk, he'd lain awake at night wondering if he really could get her riled up enough to marry him. He figured she was the kind of woman who was going to go down the aisle still denying that she was in love, especially with him. Persuading her otherwise might be challenging enough to make him forget all about bringing in another gusher.

If it turned out he was wrong about keeping his interest in Dani alive for all eternity, at least the boys would have a mom again. He would be free to get back to the kind of work he loved. Even as the unfairness and selfishness of that plan struck him, he tried to calculate how to make it work.

He felt Zack tugging on his sleeve to get his attention. "Then she would be our mom, right?"

"Yes, if it happens, she would be your mom. Would that be okay with you guys?"

Joshua shrugged. "I suppose."

Duke was startled by the less than enthusiastic endorsement. Had he read the signals all wrong again? "I thought you liked Dani," he said.

"I do, but moms go away sometimes," Josh said, fighting tears. "It might be better if Dani was just our friend."

Holy kamoley, Duke thought. This was an angle he'd never expected. He gathered both boys close.

"Not every mom goes away," he said carefully.

He'd tried very hard not to blame their mother for running out. In fact, he'd bent over backward to shoulder most of the responsibility for driving her away. If she ever came back, he didn't want the boys to hate her for something for which much of the blame was his.

He struggled for an explanation that would console and offer hope at the same time. "We've talked about this before. Sometimes things happen between grown-ups that can't be helped. When it does, one of them goes away. That doesn't mean you shouldn't love them when they're around or treasure the good memories you have. You have to take risks or you'll go through life being very lonely.''

"No way,'' Zack protested fiercely. "We've got each other. We'll never be lonely. We don't need anybody else.''

"If that were true, would you be having such a good time with your new friends here in Los Pinos?''

Both boys hesitated as they considered that.

"I guess not,'' Josh conceded.

"Someday you're going to be a grown-up, and you're going to want even more than good friends. You're going to want somebody to love. I want you to believe that taking a chance on love is worth the risk, worth whatever hurt might happen.'' He grinned at them. "Because, you know what? Sometimes that risk pays off big time and lasts forever.''

"Like with you and us,'' Joshua said.

Duke's eyes swam with unshed tears. "Exactly,'' he whispered. "Exactly like us.''

And if he had his way, Dani would become a part of that tight-knit circle just as soon as he could make it happen. Despite what he'd just told his sons about putting everything on the line for love, the only thing he wasn't willing to risk was his own heart. He'd had years of evidence to analyze. He was pretty sure he didn't even have one.

On Thanksgiving morning Dani discovered the kitchen at White Pines in predictable chaos. Maritza, who'd been Grandpa Harlan's housekeeper practically forever, was trying her best to shoo everyone out, but lured by the scent of roasting turkey and pumpkin pie, no one was paying a bit of attention. Even Janet, whose lack of culinary skills was the stuff of family legend, seemed drawn to the one room in the house she usually avoided.

"Señora Janet, everything here is under control," Maritza declared again. "Please, you go and take the others with you. It is Thanksgiving. You should be relaxing and enjoying your company."

Janet made a token protest, offered to make the dressing and was soundly discouraged not only by Maritza, but also by everyone else as well.

"Ungrateful wretches," Janet said, laughing. She scowled at Jenny. "You especially. I expected more loyalty from my firstborn daughter."

"Hey, I grew up on your cooking for the first fourteen years of my life. The best I can say is that I survived it." She turned to her younger sister. "Lizzy, you have no idea how grateful you should be that Maritza is here."

Janet threw up her hands. "Okay, enough. I'm going where I'm appreciated."

"I saw Dad out by the barn with Duke and the twins," Lizzy offered. "Dad is always eager to see you."

Janet gave them all a satisfied smile. "Yes, he is, isn't he?" she said as she slipped out the screen door.

Dani watched her go and wished she could follow. She was still putting up a valiant battle with her emotions, but she feared she was losing the war. Just the mention of Duke's name was enough to stir her senses alive. It really was absurd how little control she had over her reactions to the man. Worse, he knew it and he was deliberately plaguing her.

He never had gotten around to asking that all-important question that had brought him into her office a few weeks back. She'd been left to speculate and wonder and worry, even though he was suddenly underfoot everywhere she went. There hadn't been a doubt in her mind that someone would think to include him and the boys in today's celebration. Hearing that he was outside with her grandfather had made her pulse jump just the same.

"You could go, too," Jenny suggested mildly.

Dani stared at her. "Go where?"

"Out to the barn."

"Why would I want to do that?"

Jenny laughed. "Oh, sweetie, give it up. The only one not admitting that you're nuts about the guy is you."

Dani frowned. "One of these days, Jenny Runningbear Adams, you are going to fall head over heels in love with some man and I am going to lead the troops in making your life miserable about it."

"Not me," Jenny declared emphatically. "I don't have time to fall in love. Between lobbying in Washington and teaching, my plate is full. I'm perfectly content."

"Famous last words," Dani taunted. She glanced at Lizzy, who was listening in with an amused expression. "I say a year, tops. How about you?"

"First she has to meet somebody," Lizzy pointed out. "She never pokes her head into anyplace where she's likely to meet anyone interesting. She spends all her time surrounded by teenagers and lawyers.''

"Watch it, baby sister," Jenny warned. "Our mother is a lawyer. She wouldn't appreciate you disparaging her kind.''

"Everyone knows that Mom's an exception," Lizzy said loyally. "The ones you know are out for a buck.''

"How would you know that? You've never met most of them.''

"I hear you and Mom and Dad talking. How do you think I got to be so smart?''

Jenny chuckled. "Who says you're smart?''

"Daddy.''

Dani and Jenny exchanged a look. "Of course," Dani said. "For a minute there, we forgot we were talking to Grandpa Harlan's best and brightest.''

Lizzy scowled at her teasing. "I could tell you a few things..." she muttered.

"Such as?'' Dani asked.

"You seem to forget that I worked for Duke all summer long," Lizzy taunted meaningfully.

Dani's heart seemed to lurch to a stop. "So?''

"I heard stuff.''

"About?''

"Never mind," Lizzy said airily. "I'm going out where I'm appreciated, too.''

She left her sister and Dani staring after her.

"What do you suppose she knows?'' Dani asked, unable to mask her curiosity.

"Very little, I think," Maritza chimed in from the stove. "She is just talking big to get your attention.''

"It worked, too," Jenny observed thoughtfully. "She mentioned Duke and your antenna shot up. Interesting reaction for a woman who claims the man doesn't matter to her."

"Oh, go to hell," Dani muttered.

"Young lady, you do not use such talk in my kitchen," Maritza said indignantly. "You are not too big for me to wash out your mouth with soap."

"Uh-oh," Jenny taunted. "You're in big trouble now."

"I'm going where I'm appreciated," Dani said.

"To the barn?" Jenny asked, her eyes twinkling.

"No. To find my father."

"Now there's the ticket. Run off to Jordan," Jenny taunted. "Don't expect him to side with you, though. He's like the rest of us. He's just waiting for an engagement announcement. He discovered that being a daddy was fun. Now he wants to try out being a granddaddy."

"He does not," Dani protested, though the claim made her very nervous. She suspected there might be some truth to it.

"Does, too."

"*Niñas,* stop it," Maritza ordered. "You will spoil the food with all this bickering. Be nice."

Dani laughed. "How often have we heard those words?" she asked as she wrapped her arms around Maritza and hugged her. "*Te amo,* Maritza."

The housekeeper's dour expression softened. "*Te amo,* Danielle. You are my own precious one."

"I thought I was," Jenny protested with a glint of pure mischief in her eyes.

"You, *niña*, are the thorn in my side, especially today. Now go. You both are in my way."

It seemed everywhere Dani went she was in the way. She tried the den, but Jordan, Cody and Luke were busy cussing a blue streak at the television. It appeared the Dallas Cowboys weren't delivering today.

Restless, it was probably inevitable that she would wander out to the barn. She swore it had nothing at all to do with Duke's presence out there. Everyone was there, after all. Not just the man who made her toes tingle and tempted her to forget every resolution she'd made about choosing more wisely the next time she fell in love.

She also swore that she wouldn't have gravitated directly toward him, if it hadn't been for Joshua and Zachary. They rushed over and each clasped a hand, drawing her straight toward their father.

"Tell her, Dad. Tell her about the horses you're gonna get us," Joshua said, practically jumping up and down with excitement.

Dani met Duke's gaze and felt that increasingly familiar jolt of excitement, the unmistakable tug that would have had a less stubborn woman throwing herself into his arms. She was almost used to it now. At least, it no longer left her thoroughly tongue-tied.

"If you're thinking of getting them horses, I gather they've passed the pet test?" she said to him.

"It's been months now, and the cats are still alive," he said dryly. "It's a small victory for responsibility." He regarded her speculatively. "You know, I'm going to need some help with this one."

"What kind of help?"

"Picking out the right horses, checking into their breeding, going over them to make sure they're sound. You're a vet. You'll be much better at that than I would be," he said, then added a little too casually, "Think you could carve out a little time and go with me to a horse sale?"

Dani was flattered that he trusted her judgment, but going off to a horse sale with him meant spending time alone, just the two of them. She suspected from the gleam in his eyes that finding the best animals for his money wasn't the only thing on his mind.

For weeks now Duke had done nothing to alarm her. He hadn't even given her more than a chaste peck on the cheek. Still, she was smart enough to realize that the growing lust she was feeling wasn't entirely one-sided. A few hours cooped up in a car and who knew what ideas he might get.

Not that she didn't trust him, she told herself. It was herself she didn't trust. The very sensible reasons she'd had for resisting Duke were fading, lost in a haze of pure longing that was deepening over time.

She forced herself to try once more to beg off. "Duke, I'm more than happy to give you some pointers, but I'd hate to be responsible for the final decision. It's your money."

"I'll be taken to the cleaners," he insisted. "They'll see me coming a mile away."

"Then take my father or Uncle Cody," she said, unsuccessfully trying to fight the note of desperation that was creeping into her voice. "Heck, Grandpa Harlan would love to go. There's nothing he likes more than a good horse sale and a chance to do some bargaining.''

"I want your help," he insisted.

The man could match any Adams she knew for pure cussedness, she concluded with a sigh. "Why me?" she asked.

"You aren't scared to spend the day with me, are you?" he retorted.

Her temper flared with predictable speed at the taunt. "Of course not."

"You sure about that, darlin? You sound scared."

"Oh, for heaven's sakes, when is this sale?"

"Next weekend."

"Where?"

"Fort Worth."

It would be a long trip, but it could be done in a day, Dani reassured herself. They would be surrounded by hordes of people for most of that time. What could happen? Nothing, absolutely nothing. Not if she didn't allow it. Maybe it was time to put her resolutions to the test. She sighed.

"What time do you want to go?"

"I'll pick you up at five, so we'll have time to look the horses over before the sale starts."

She studied his face intently. His expression was pure innocence, but there was a glint in his eyes that suggested he was gloating. After all, he had gotten his way. Again. Why shouldn't he gloat? She had the resistance of a limp noodle where he was concerned.

"Can we come, too?" Joshua pleaded.

As if he'd forgotten his sons' presence and the purpose of the trip to Fort Worth, Duke blinked and stared at Joshua for a full minute before shaking his head.

"No," he said flatly.

"But, Dad..." Zack protested.

"I said no," Duke repeated.

"The horses are for us," Zack argued.

"Yes, they are," Dani agreed, siding with the boys for her own less than honorable purposes. "They should have some say."

"Coward," Duke murmured just for her ears.

Since she couldn't deny it, she pretended she hadn't even heard. "Well?" she said. "Can they come?"

"No, indeed, they can't go," her grandfather said, stepping into the fray at the most inopportune moment possible. "I have plans for you two boys right here."

"But..." Joshua began.

"No buts," her grandfather said firmly. "No point in picking out horses, if you can't ride. While your daddy and Dani are off in Fort Worth, Cody and I will give you your first lessons."

To Dani's dismay, both boys reacted with enthusiasm. So much for her salvation. This time when she met Duke's gaze, there was no mistaking the triumph. Since Maritza wasn't nearby to reproach her, she told him to go to hell, too.

He laughed. "Been there, darlin'. This time I'm aiming for heaven."

Chapter Eleven

It was pitch-dark outside, the kind of velvet blanket of darkness that made a person want to snuggle up next to a lover and light up the night with emotional fireworks.

Dani stood in the doorway, a cup of very strong coffee in her hands, and tried to dismiss from her thoughts the provocative image she'd just created. It was virtually impossible, especially since Duke seemed to be the lover crowded into that image with her.

It was barely four-thirty and she was already dressed and far too eager for their trip to Fort Worth. A dozen excuses for staying home had popped to the tip of her tongue since Thanksgiving, but she hadn't uttered a one of them. Either she was totally and unredeemably reckless or she was deluding herself about the power of the attraction between her and Duke.

When bright headlights cut through the darkness at the end of the block, her nerves kicked in. At this hour there was no question of it being anyone other than Duke. Since he was early, she could only assume he was as anxious as she was about whatever lay ahead.

She already knew that he'd made arrangements to drop Josh and Zack off at White Pines the night before. For some reason the evidence of his eagerness seemed to calm her just a little. He was usually so confident, so blasted sure of himself. It was nice to see a little hint of vulnerability for a change.

As he pulled to a stop, she stood her ground, watching, waiting to see what note he would strike when he greeted her. Casual and easy? Provocative? Maybe daring?

Her pulse skittered crazily as she anticipated his lips settling on hers for what he meant to be a cool, friendly greeting. Both of them knew by now that no amount of control or caution could tame a real kiss between them. It was why he'd deliberately dusted the air by her cheek and forehead for weeks now. Even innocent kisses had a way of turning stunningly sexual in an instant.

"Hey, darlin', are you ready?" he called out without leaving the car.

Fighting a ridiculous sense of disappointment, she forced a smile. "I'll be right there. Would you like some coffee for the road?"

He held up a covered mug. "Already have it.

There's another one here for you, along with a bag of doughnuts fresh from the oven. I threw myself on Sallie's mercy over at the bakery, and she slipped me a few out the back door.''

Dani had a hunch Sallie hadn't required much persuading. She was a sucker for a handsome face. Always had been, even though she'd been happily married to the same man for almost fifty years now. Sallie was every bit as much of a flirt as Betty Lou. Every man in town knew they could sweet-talk her into tucking an extra doughnut in the bag every now and again.

Dani took one last look at the cats' lineup of bowls in the kitchen to make sure they were all full, then grabbed her jacket and purse and locked the front door behind her.

When she reached the car, Duke leaned across the front seat and opened the door for her.

"No overnight bag?" he inquired.

Her alarmed gaze flew to his, but she managed to keep her voice even. "We're coming back tonight," she said firmly. "That was the plan."

"Well, of course, it is," he agreed at once. "But you know how unpredictable the weather can be this time of year. I've brought one. It never hurts to be prepared for plans to go awry."

"Ours won't," Dani stated grimly.

Duke grinned. "I'll be sure to pass along your conviction to the weatherman."

She studied him through narrowed eyes. "Do you know something about the weather that I don't?" she asked, cursing herself for not checking out the eleven o'clock news the night before or the weather channel this morning. For all she knew a blizzard could be headed for Texas, and they were driving straight into it. If getting stranded suited Duke's purposes, she wondered if he would bother to mention an approaching storm.

"Maybe I ought to check the weather channel before we take off," she said, reaching for the door handle.

"No need. They're just predicting a little rain around Fort Worth. It shouldn't be a problem," he said blandly, pulling out of the driveway before Dani had a chance to evaluate whether the rain presented a real danger.

"Just rain?" she asked.

He shrugged. "Unless the temperature drops."

She didn't like the way he was hedging or the way he was avoiding her gaze. "Maybe we should do this another time."

"Darlin', they're just calling for a little rain," he protested. "What's the worst that could happen? We'd have to stay overnight. We're both adults. That shouldn't be a problem, right?"

No, it shouldn't be, Dani agreed to herself. But it would be. She could feel it in her bones...and elsewhere.

"I don't know—" she began.

"Trust me, darlin', we'll be just fine. Now sit back and relax. Drink your coffee before it gets cold and try one of these doughnuts." He gestured to the bag on the seat between them. "There are jelly-filled, glazed and old-fashioned."

The bag was huge, big enough to hold at least a baker's dozen, though there were far fewer than that left. The assortment had clearly been plundered. Dani couldn't help grinning. "Just how many have you eaten already?"

"A couple," he said, then grinned guiltily. "Okay, maybe four. I never get to have doughnuts anymore. I'm trying to teach the boys to eat a healthy breakfast by setting a good example. I've eaten enough bran flakes in the last year to fulfill my fiber quota for two lifetimes."

"You know, an occasional doughnut won't kill any of you," Dani said. "Maybe if you ate them in moderation, you wouldn't be pigging out now."

"Darlin', I don't need a lecture on my eating habits from you."

"If you say so," she said, peering into the bag. The aroma of dough and sugar and raspberry jelly hit her smack in the face. She drew in a deep breath. "Oh, my."

"Downright intoxicating, isn't it?" Duke teased.

"Incredible," she murmured distractedly. All of her attention was focused on the choice she was about to make.

"You could have one of each," Duke said, clearly guessing her dilemma.

"I couldn't," she insisted and settled for the raspberry-filled doughnut that was still warm to the touch. Powdered sugar coated her lips. Jam settled in the corners of her mouth and left her fingers sticky. "Heavenly."

Duke glanced over at her, then sucked in a sharp breath. Pure lust darkened his eyes.

"What?" Dani demanded, her own breath catching.

"There are napkins in the glove compartment," Duke said in a choked voice.

"Why? Am I a mess?"

"Not exactly," he said. "But if you don't wipe away the sugar and jam around your mouth, I'm going to have to do it for you." His heated gaze clashed with hers. "I won't be using a napkin."

The image of his tongue searching out every little trace of sugar and jam slammed into her with the force of a gale. She fumbled badly as she tried to open the glove compartment and retrieve a napkin. Her hand shook as she tried to wipe away any trace of the doughnut she had savored.

"Too bad," Duke teased when she was done. "I was looking forward to helping."

"I'll just bet you were," she said. A change of topic was definitely in order. "Why don't you tell me what you have in mind when it comes to the horses. How much do you want to spend? Is there any particular type of horse you want?"

He chuckled. "Smooth transition. Don't tell me I was making you nervous."

"You weren't," she insisted.

"Liar."

She regarded him impatiently. "Duke, you asked me to come along today to help you buy horses. That's all I'm doing here."

"I know," he said.

She didn't trust that dutiful tone one bit. "I hope you do."

He sketched a cross over his heart. "Darlin', if you made yourself any clearer, I'd have a knot upside my head."

"Don't tempt me."

"Damn, but you're cute when—"

She scowled at him. "Don't say it. Don't you dare say it."

"You want me to be honest, don't you?"

"Of course, but—"

"That's all I'm doing. Telling it like it is."

Dani sighed heavily. "Why don't I believe that?"

"You have a suspicious nature," he suggested.

"My nature, as you put it, has been honed by experience."

"You're not comparing me to that Rob person again, are you?" He didn't wait for her reply. "I'm disappointed. I thought we were way beyond that."

"Well, we're not," she grumbled. "You're sneaky and underhanded, just like he was."

"Me? Name one single sneaky, underhanded thing I've done."

Naturally, every one she came up with sounded petty, so she kept her mouth clamped firmly shut.

"Cat got your tongue?" he inquired.

"No the cat does not have my tongue," she snapped. "I'm just trying to be civil. Otherwise this is going to be a very long trip."

Duke's eyes were flashing with humor. "Hey, don't stand on ceremony on my account. Say whatever's on your mind and get it out of your system. I can take it."

She turned to face him. "Okay, don't say you didn't ask for it."

"I'm ready," he said, his expression stoic.

Suddenly, the list of his so-called sins seemed endless. She couldn't wait to enumerate them all.

"From the day we met you have been trying to disrupt my life," she accused. "You turn up everywhere I go like the proverbial bad penny. You've deliberately ingratiated yourself with my family. They all think you hung the moon. They're plotting and scheming on your behalf without the slightest regard for my feelings."

"That's not the way they see it," Duke pointed out.

"Well, of course, it isn't. They're a bunch of softhearted romantics. Grandpa Harlan is the worst of all. I thought I could count on my father being on my side, but even he seems to have joined the enemy camp. As for your boys, they have managed to slip past my best defenses."

His eyebrows rose at that. "Now there's a crime."

"Lay off. You asked me to say what was on my mind."

"So I did. Do go on."

"You don't listen to a word I say."

"I listen to every single word you say," Duke protested. "It's just that sometimes you and I may disagree on whether or not you mean what you say."

"Of course, I mean it," she practically shouted.

"Do you think I'm just wasting my breath for the heck of it?"

Duke shook his head and regarded her with something she suspected was awfully close to pity. She felt like slugging him.

"Of course not," he soothed. "The logical, rational side of your brain means every word. I'm not so dense that I'd miss a thing like that."

"Then what's the problem?" she demanded.

He reached over and touched a finger lightly to the center of her chest. "That's the problem," he said gently. "Your heart and your brain aren't in sync. Sharon Lynn and Jenny see it. Your father and grandfather see it. Now, I may not understand a lot about women. I may know even less about emotions, but I do get one thing. When push comes to shove, it's what your heart feels that really matters."

Dani felt the very organ in question pump a little faster as if to confirm what he said. She'd been so sure that he couldn't see through her, so sure that she could keep her secret, forever if she had to. Then, *wham,* just like that it was all over. The truth was out or would be, if she confirmed his suspicions.

She just couldn't do it. She settled for lying, instead, in a valiant attempt to save herself—to save them—from making a terrible mistake.

"You're wrong," she said quietly, but emphatically. "You have it all wrong."

It would have been enough to convince any other man. Or at least any other man would have graciously accepted the lie and let things be. Not Duke. He just smiled knowingly.

"If you say so, darlin'."

"Don't use that patronizing tone with me," she said, fuming.

He seemed even more amused by the outburst. "Sorry," he apologized with a total lack of sincerity.

Dani shook her head and bit back another sharp retort that he would only find even more unconvincing.

"Hey, don't worry about it. We'll work it out."

"We will not work it out," she said, her teeth clenched.

"Sure we will. You may be an Adams, but I'm every bit as stubborn."

Now there, she thought dispiritedly, was the truth. The realization scared her to death.

Duke thought the drive had gone very well. Dani was so furious steam was practically spewing out of her ears. That was good. It meant he was getting to her, shaking her up, rattling her. Anytime now he would get her to make an honest admission of her feelings toward him. He'd thought for a minute she was about to blurt it out, but then she'd sucked in a deep breath and gone all stiff and silent on him. He could have told her that was every bit as telling, but wisely he didn't. She was in no mood to appreciate the observation.

He supposed he ought to feel guilty about backing her into a corner, but he needed her to acknowledge what she felt. So he had to move on to the next stage of his plan: getting her to say yes to a marriage proposal.

He glanced over at her as they pulled into a parking place behind the barns where the horse sale was being held. Her hands were clenched together so tightly in her lap that her knuckles were white. He had a feeling if he laid his hands on her shoulders, he would find knots of tension as big as Texas...right before she throttled him for touching her.

"Are you planning on speaking to me ever again?" he inquired lightly. "If not, exactly how are you going to communicate with me when you spot the perfect horse?"

Her lips twitched ever so slightly. "I was thinking of kicking you real hard in the shins."

He grinned. "That would get my attention, that's for sure."

"I wonder," she said.

His gaze narrowed. "What's that supposed to mean?"

"It means I'm not sure that a baseball bat to the head would get your attention unless you wanted it to."

"I am single-minded," he agreed. "You probably need to remember that."

"Believe me, it's not something I'm likely to forget," she retorted. "Now are we going to sit here all day or are we going to check out the horses?"

He went around the car and opened her door with a flourish. "Lead the way, darlin'. There's nothing I like better than following along behind a pretty woman."

She scowled at the remark and, he noticed, made darn sure that she was always beside him and not in front of him. With brisk efficiency, she found the listings of the horses for sale and scanned the pages, checking several and crossing off twice as many.

"Let's go," she said, studying the arrangement of the stalls. "There's a pinto pony in number seventy-six that might be just right."

When they found it, Duke took one look at the skittish animal and concluded it had been rounded up wild and half-starved to death before being brought to today's sale. As Dani approached, fear darkened the horse's eyes and made them flare dangerously.

"Dani," Duke said very softly. "Careful."

She nodded, acknowledging the warning. Then she reached in her pocket for a lump of sugar and held it out. The pony shied away from her. Dani eased closer, murmuring nonsense until eventually the pony remained still when she approached. Duke's heart stayed in his throat the whole time. He was fairly sure he didn't breathe again until Dani backed out of reach of the horse's nervous hooves.

"That horse has been mistreated," Duke said angrily when she was beside him again. "You're lucky he didn't kick you."

"He's malnourished, that's for sure," she agreed, her eyes wide and shimmering with tears. "But he's beautiful, Duke. He's full of life."

"He's too skittish for the boys."

"He wouldn't be if someone cared for him," she argued.

"Dani, he's the first horse we've seen. Hold off on a recommendation until we've seen the rest that you've marked."

She faced him stubbornly. "He's going to stay on the list," she insisted. "You'll see."

Duke sighed, relieved that he'd borrowed a horse trailer large enough to carry half a dozen horses. He had a feeling Dani was going to be an easy mark. If he didn't agree with her selections, she would probably buy the others herself.

They looked over another eleven horses. Out of the even dozen she'd selected, she found four she thought were both sound and likely to go for the right price. Not counting that blasted pinto, of course. That made five she considered worth bidding on.

"Which one of us is going to bid?" she asked Duke when it was time for the sale to begin. "You should since it's your money we're spending."

"I'm sticking with you," he insisted. "You know the value of these horses better than I do. I'm liable to get carried away."

She regarded him doubtfully. "You don't strike me as the kind of man who'd get carried away at an auction."

"Why not?"

"Too hardheaded," she said succinctly. "You'd be more likely to set a figure and stick with it, no matter how badly you wanted the horse."

To be perfectly truthful, she was right, Duke admitted, but only to himself. At least that's how he always had been. Today, though, he had the feeling that he could very easily get caught up in Dani's excitement and lose his head completely. In fact, he was already more than half certain that they would be leaving with that pinto if he had to buy it for her himself. She hadn't stopped talking about it since they'd first visited the horse's stall. He had a feeling buying it would be the kind of outrageous gesture no one had ever made for her before. Maybe it would prove to be the clincher in his plan.

There were two palominos early in the sale, practically mirror images of each other. Duke knew that Dani was leaning toward them for the boys. He'd liked them himself. They appeared gentle enough.

In the guise of having her show him what she was looking for when she examined them, he'd gone over them himself and confirmed Dani's view that they were strong and sound. When he'd commented on just that, she'd regarded him with an odd expression on her face. He'd warned himself to be very careful. One more mistake like that would be his downfall. Dani was too smart not to catch on sooner or later that he knew exactly what he was doing. Then there was going to be big trouble. He was resigned to it.

In the meantime, though, he had her to himself for an entire day. She'd stopped being skittish hours ago. She'd even laughed at a few of his jokes and reached for his hand on one occasion, only to drop it like a branding iron when she realized what she'd done.

When the first of the palominos came on the block, the bidding was fairly light. Dani picked the horse up for well under the limit Duke had set. She flashed a look of triumph at him at the conclusion of the bidding.

"This is fun," she announced. "No wonder Grandpa Harlan loves horse-trading so much. I hope we can get the second one, too." Her eyes darkened with worry. "Or do you think the boys would rather have horses that don't look alike? Are they sensitive about the twin thing?"

Duke had never given the matter much thought. Even though they were identical, they'd never been dressed exactly alike or given the same toys. They had surprisingly individual tastes and interests. Their personalities were a blend of harmony and diversity. At times, they acted as one. At other times, they behaved like any other squabbling, jealous non-twin siblings.

"My hunch is the only way to avoid conflict might be to give them matching horses," he told her. "This is a pretty big deal. We don't want either of them getting the idea that the other's horse is better in some way you and I don't get."

Dani grinned sympathetically. "Figuring out how eight-year-olds think does have its moments, doesn't it?"

"I'm sure it has brought many a parent to his knees," Duke agreed. "Go for the other palomino."

"I agree. Maybe if they both weren't so beautiful, I'd go a different way, but they're gorgeous."

"You don't think this second one is going to have a problem with that left front foreleg, do you?"

She shot him a suspicious look. "What are you talking about?"

Careful, Duke warned himself. "It seemed to me his gait was a little off. You mentioned it yourself, didn't you?"

Dani scanned her notes. "I did write it down," she agreed, but she was clearly unsettled by his observation. "I don't think it's a problem, though. I've seen other horses like that do just fine. If it comes to that, it's a correctible problem with fairly minor surgery. If you wanted more than a riding horse, we should probably reconsider, but for Josh or Zack, the palomino will get along okay."

Duke nodded. "I'll trust your judgment."

The bidding for the second palomino was livelier than the first, proving that plenty of others were just as unconcerned as Dani about the horse's unusual gait. When they neared Duke's preset limit, Dani glanced over at him.

"Well?"

He grinned. "Go up, if you have to. The other one was a steal. It'll all even out."

"All right," she said and reentered the bidding frenzy with enthusiasm.

Naturally, she triumphed, Duke was holding his breath on the last round. Not that he couldn't afford to spend more. He could. He just wasn't sure the horse was worth it. The beaming smile on Dani's face, however, was worth every penny.

"That's it, then," he said when the bidding was done. "Mission accomplished."

"Not quite," she said.

"Let me guess. The pinto."

"I have to have him," she said. "He needs a good home."

"Do you have room in your backyard?" Duke inquired dryly.

She shot him a we-are-not-amused look. "There's plenty of room at Mom and Dad's," she said.

"And you get out there how often?"

"Do you really have to be so blasted logical?" she inquired testily.

Duke threw back his head and laughed at that. She grinned and admitted, "Okay, it's like the pot calling the kettle black. I want that horse."

Duke nodded. "I know. His number won't be up for a while now. Want to go grab a bite to eat?"

"Sure."

He led the way to a vendor selling hot dogs and soft drinks. Dani slathered her hot dog with mustard, relish and was debating over the onions when he caught her eye. She swallowed hard, then left the onions untouched. He figured it was tantamount to an admission that she knew before the day ended they would share at least one kiss, probably more.

They finished their meal and were about to go back inside, when Duke caught a glimpse of the dab of mustard at the corner of her mouth. All of the desire that had rocketed through him that morning when she'd been eating that doughnut came back now with twice the intensity.

"Wait," he said softly and reached for a napkin. Alarm flared in her eyes as he tilted her chin up. His thumb skimmed her lower lip, even as he gently wiped away the mustard with the napkin.

"Thanks." It came out as a breathless whisper.

"No problem," he said, though it was a lie. There was a very definite problem. He suddenly wanted nothing more than to drag her off somewhere and tumble her into a haystack or a bed or any other place that would be soft and accommodating.

As if the gods had heard his prayers, a flash of lightning split the sky, followed by a clap of thunder. The skies opened up and rain came down, first in huge, individual drops, then in solid gray sheets. Duke grabbed Dani's hand, and they made a dash back inside.

Fortunately, they'd been quick enough to avoid being soaked to the skin. Duke glanced over her. "You okay? We could leave if you're too wet. There's no point in catching pneumonia."

"Nice try, but I am not leaving without my horse," she said stubbornly.

Quite a few of the other serious bidders caught a glimpse of the storm and decided to flee before it got any worse. When the pinto's number was called, the hall was half-empty. Dani had only one competitor for the horse, and he was bidding with lackluster enthusiasm. He dropped out after only four rounds.

Eyes shining, Dani turned to Duke. "I stole him. I virtually stole him."

"I just hope the payback for your thievery isn't a broken neck," Duke retorted.

"A lot you know," she countered. "That horse is going to be the best investment I ever made."

"Obviously, you've never heard of stocks and bonds," he countered.

"Oh, give it up," she said finally and flashed a knowing smile at him. "Otherwise I might make you explain why it is that you claimed not to know anything about horses, when it's obvious that you know at least as much as I do. I might have taken classes in vet school, but you've spent time around horses, haven't you?''

Uh-oh, Duke thought. "You figured it out, huh?"

"Hours ago. Next time you decide to feign ignorance, it might be a real good idea to keep your mouth shut," she advised.

"I was hoping you'd think I just happened to ask particularly intelligent questions."

"Not just intelligent questions, *well-informed* questions. There's a difference."

"Are you going to hold it against me?"

"Not if you'll tell me why you lied about knowing anything about horses."

"Isn't that obvious?"

"Not to me."

He reached out and touched a finger to her cheek. His gaze locked with hers as he confessed, "It was the only way I could come up with to get you alone for an entire day."

"Oh."

He smiled at that. Oh, indeed. He wondered what she'd think if she figured out he'd been praying to beat the band that this rain would turn to ice any second now so they would be stranded overnight, too.

As if to prove that he still had some pull with heaven, hail began pinging against the cars and trailers outside, making an unmistakable clatter.

Dani's eyes widened as she recognized the implication. "Hail?"

"Sounds like it."

"Maybe it'll pass," she suggested hopefully.

"Do you want to take that chance?" he asked reasonably.

She looked torn. Clearly, she was indecisive about which danger was the greatest—going or staying. She lifted her gaze to his and he could read those by-now familiar warring emotions, desire and panic.

"I'll trust your judgment," she said quietly.

As she said it, her gaze never wavered.

And Duke felt the full weight of responsibility settling on his shoulders. She was leaving more than their going or staying up to him, and they both knew it. He would also be the one to decide if tonight was the night they finally made love.

He could make her respond, make her forget her reservations about their relationship with just a kiss. It would be a simple matter to seduce her...if he dared. Whatever he decided, he would have to live with the decision forever after.

Chapter Twelve

She could live with this, Dani told herself staunchly as Duke drove through the blinding combination of rain and sleet in search of a decent-looking motel. They were adults. Nothing was going to happen beyond getting a good night's sleep unless they both wanted it to.

Unless, of course, her hormones overruled her head, she thought grimly. Maybe she should play it safe and put up more of a fight to go straight back to Los Pinos. She glanced at Duke's tense expression. When he gazed over at her and gave her a quick smile, she felt her pulse zing dangerously. Suddenly, a tactical retreat seemed like a very good idea.

"Are you certain we can't get back tonight?" she asked, peering out the window at the leaden sky. "It looks as if it might clear up," she added with unjustified optimism based on a pinprick-sized patch of blue in the distance.

"Do you believe in the tooth fairy, too?" Duke inquired, not taking his eyes from the hazardous road.

"You don't have to be sarcastic," she said, but she could see his point. The road already had an inch or more of swirling water on it, more than enough to send a car off in a skid and dangerously close to enough to have it stall out. Despite that tiny bit of blue, most of the sky was filled with stormy, rain-filled clouds.

"Why don't you help me out by looking for a half-decent place to stay," Duke suggested. "I passed one motel a block back, but it looked like a dump."

Dani had seen it, too. To describe it as seedy-looking would have been a compliment. Duke would have had to drag her kicking and screaming into a place that crummy. "You drive. I'll look," she said resignedly.

It took another fifteen minutes before she spotted a motel with a Rooms Available sign lit and a small, cozy-looking restaurant attached. It wasn't exactly a luxury resort, but it would do. Perhaps even more important from her perspective, there wasn't the slightest suggestion of a romantic retreat about it, at least if taste was any factor at all. It was very much bright lights and gaudy ambience.

"How about that one?" she asked. "It looks clean."

Duke followed the direction of her gaze. His expression turned skeptical. "You don't mind the flashing neon and the water-bed option?"

"The water bed is just that, an option," she said firmly, even though her stomach turned flip-flops at the thought of climbing into one with Duke. "As for the neon, who cares what's flashing outside. We'll be asleep."

"Your choice," he said and swung the car into the parking lot. "I'll see what's available."

"Duke?"

"Yes?"

"Skip the water bed. I want an ordinary mattress."

"All to yourself?" he inquired, his tone light.

She thought about it for no longer than a heartbeat, but apparently that was long enough for him to interpret the message of uncertainty.

"I'll get two rooms," Duke said, taking the decision out of her hands.

If he was upset, he didn't show it. Still, Dani stared after him, already regretting her cowardice. Would it be so awful to steal just one night with this man?

The answer to that was a straightforward, unequivocal yes. One night would never be enough. Despite her very best efforts, he had gotten to her. She had ignored danger signs, alarms and warning bells. She had allowed herself to fall for him—and for his kids—but it wasn't going to work.

Not for lack of interest, of course. Duke wanted her. She wasn't mistaken about that. He also considered her good mother material. She had recognized that as well. But he didn't love her. There was a part of himself he always held back, even when he was flirting the most outrageously. In the end, that inability to love her wholeheartedly was all that really mattered. She wouldn't settle for less than the surrender of his heart.

Of course, she, too, was holding back, she reminded herself. It made them quite a pair.

She peered disconsolately out the window just in time to see Duke dashing back to the car. His clothes were soaked. Water dripped from his hair and ran down his face. He looked as if he'd just climbed from a shower with his clothes on. The image sent heat shimmering through her.

Duke, however, was shivering. "Bad news, darlin'. There's only one room left. We're going to have to share."

Dani's heart began to hammer. She couldn't demand that they search for someplace else. They'd passed almost every motel within miles of the horse show. They were either shabby or fully occupied. Duke was too soaked to be driving around anymore, anyway. Fate, it seemed, had stepped in.

"It has two beds, though," he said as he pulled up in front of the room at the very end of the row facing the street.

Dani blinked and stared, taken aback by the belated announcement. "What did you say?"

"Not to worry. It has two beds."

Relief washed over her, followed almost instantly by disappointment. The latter, combined with a healthy dose of frustration, made her cranky.

Reluctantly, she followed Duke, coming to an abrupt halt just inside the doorway. There were two beds, all right, both of them seductively huge. The motel might have an uninspired, gaudy exterior, but the rooms themselves were generously sized and decorated with expensive, but still garish taste. There was a lot of red, she noted, with a startling dash of purple thrown in. Through the open doorway she could see that the bathroom was tiled in a vivid pink.

Duke caught her expression and grinned. "If you think this is bright, you should meet Mrs. Perez at the registration desk. She's wearing an outfit that would blind anyone without sunglasses. She says everyone needs color in their lives. It cheers them up."

He crossed the room to stand in front of her. "Are you feeling cheered up?"

"Not exactly," she said, though she was rapidly getting there. She made one last desperate pitch for sanity. "Are you absolutely sure we couldn't make it back home?"

Duke didn't appear to mind the question. He seemed to sense her need for reassurance.

"Absolutely," he said emphatically. "It's pouring rain, mixed with hail. Another hour of these plummeting temperatures and the roads will be sheets of ice. I don't want to take a chance skidding on the highway while I'm trailering three horses back home. We'll pick them up in the morning and get an early start. Maybe the weather will break by then."

"And maybe it won't," she observed. "Then what? You going to settle down in Fort Worth?"

"You ever known it to rain for months on end in Texas?"

"No, but I've never known a man to be scared by a little shower before, either."

"Darlin', we made the right decision. Mrs. Perez

says a tornado touched down not twenty miles north of here. You can't see across the road. This isn't a little, inconvenient shower we can wait out. It's a full-blown winter storm and way too unpredictable to be on the road.''

"Whatever you say."

The truth was she was having a full-scale attack of jitters. Ever since she'd gotten a look at those beds and all that provocative red, she'd felt caught up in an irresistible web of sensuality. In the pit of her stomach, she had that hovering-on-the-edge sensation that the room itself was just daring her to behave wickedly.

Given her own sadly deficient resistance, she told herself she didn't want to spend the night within fifty miles of this man, not with the spark of pure lust she'd been spying in his eyes these past months. Heck, in these past few minutes.

Worse, she suspected it was reflected in her own eyes. The man made her hotter than West Texas pavement in the midday August sun, she conceded as Duke went into the bathroom and turned the shower on.

He stuck his head out the door. "Sure you don't want to join me?" he inquired, regarding her hopefully.

"Very sure," she lied.

"I won't take long," he promised. "Then I'll put on some dry clothes and we can have dinner. The restaurant stays open until eight. Mrs. Perez says it has the best Tex-Mex in this part of town. Her husband's the cook.''

"Could be she's prejudiced."

He winked. "I wandered in and got a whiff of what's on the menu. Could be she's right. The aroma was downright decadent. It made my mouth water."

There was nothing Dani liked better than fiery Tex-Mex. Maybe that heat would take her mind off the steam being generated in this motel room. "That'll give me something to look forward to, then," she said.

He grinned. "I thought spending the night all alone with me would be temptation enough," he taunted, then closed the door in her face before she could respond.

Why did he have to be right? she wondered with a wistful sigh. She didn't want to be attracted to Duke Jenkins. She sure as heck hadn't wanted to kiss him, the first time or the last or any of the times in between.

Okay, let's be honest here, she corrected. She had wanted to experiment with one little kiss, but she hadn't wanted to like it. She'd wanted to hate it. She'd wanted to be so turned off that she would never, ever be tempted to throw herself into his arms the way she was right this minute. In that state of mind how could she ignore the pull of those mammoth beds? One kiss now and it would be all over, except for the morning-after regrets.

She'd lost count of the exact number of times he'd managed to steal a kiss since they'd met. She just knew it was enough to make sure she craved them. She'd moved them straight to the top of her list of things to avoid at all costs, way, way above hot fudge sundaes.

Which just proved how totally and thoroughly perverse she was. She knew the pitfalls of a relationship with a man like Duke. Ironically, she had conceded now that he was nothing like Rob. He probably wouldn't dump her on a whim without the slightest consideration of his boys. In fact, he was very much a single father whose first obligation was always going to be to his sons. And at the moment, what he wanted most to give them was a mom. In fact, she suspected that at least fifty percent of his actions lately had been calculated to claiming her not for himself, but for them. Making her the substitute mom for his kids would create a strong bond, but not strong enough to withstand the lure of another woman he might someday decide he wanted all for himself.

Nobody knew the danger of playing with that particular fire better than she did. That didn't seem to stop her from shivering like a wisp of grass in the wind every single time he touched her. Thinking about him only a few feet away, naked, was enough to send shock waves through her.

He was going to touch her tonight, too. Any minute, in fact. She just knew it, knew it with the certainty of a woman who was head over heels in love and searching for signs and portents in every single glance and innocent caress.

He was going to brush one of those oh-so-casual kisses across her forehead. She was going to subconsciously moisten her lips and then, *wham,* his mouth was going to slant across hers, and there would be no

stopping what happened next. Pent-up sexual frustration had a way of exploding sooner or later. This was
definitely later, which meant the explosion was likely
to be of atomic proportions.

Duke started his shower with the water as hot as
he could stand it, hoping to chase away the chill that
had cut all the way through to his bones. It didn't
heat him nearly as fast as thinking about Dani being
right outside the door, maybe resting on one of those
impossibly huge beds.

He chuckled at the memory of her expression when
she'd seen them. She'd looked flabbergasted, panicky
and then, in surprisingly short order, wistful. He took
the last as a very good sign.

Not that she wasn't sending out more mixed signals
than an inexperienced Ham radio operator. He knew
in his gut that it wasn't a question of her being indecisive. He figured she'd already made up her mind
that she wanted to make love. She just hadn't figured
out how to deal with the aftermath, the inevitable,
unspoken questions that always tumbled through a
woman's mind when she wasn't sure where a relationship was headed.

Duke figured he had enough answers for both of
them. This wasn't going to be a one-night stand, if
that's what she feared. It was simply going to seal
their fate, tie up the deal like a signature on a contract.
He would go home from Fort Worth with two palominos, one skittish pinto and a fiancée.

"Now, that's romantic," he muttered under his

breath. "Tell her that and you can kiss marriage goodbye."

Fortunately, he'd had the foresight to plan the rest of their evening with more care. He'd done more than peek into that restaurant. He'd spoken to Mr. Perez and planned an evening that would bring tears to her eyes and, with any luck at all, melt her heart.

By the time they got to the restaurant, there would be a bouquet of fresh flowers to replace the artificial ones on the table. Instead of a dripping red candle in an old wine jug, there would be half a dozen thick white candles casting a glow from fancy silver holders. Mr. Perez said the family had brought many pieces of fine silver from Mexico, and they would be happy to share them on such a night. And, yes, he had the perfect bottle of champagne. Like his wife, Mr. Perez had the soul of a romantic. He'd understood immediately what Duke was after.

"Very big night, *sí?*"

"Very big," Duke had agreed. The most important of his life.

Just thinking about the dinner and his plans for after raised his body temperature to a shade under unbearable. Suddenly, he had to shut off the hot water and replace it with cold. Which meant he left the shower right back where he'd started, chilled to the bone and shivering.

He wrapped a towel around his waist and stepped back into the room to grab his clothes. At the sight of Dani sitting cross-legged in the middle of the bed, her eyes glued to the TV, he halted in his tracks.

"What the hell are you watching?" he demanded as he glimpsed bodies writhing on the screen.

"Cable," she said, her voice breathless and vaguely stunned.

Choking back a chuckle, he inquired lightly, "X-rated cable, by any chance?"

She nodded, but never looked away from the screen. Duke didn't dare follow her gaze for more than a flash. Too many images like the one on-screen, and they would never get out of the room for dinner.

Dani tilted her head to follow the unlikely angle of the action. "Can you imagine?" she murmured.

"Dani?"

"Hmm?"

"Turn it off."

Her head snapped up, eyes wide. "What?"

"Turn it off," Duke said in a choked voice.

"But why?"

She studied him intently. Duke recognized the precise instant when she noticed his arousal. Suddenly, she grinned impishly.

"It's very educational," she told him.

"Any education you need along those lines, I'll be glad to give you firsthand."

Color bloomed in her cheeks. That wistful expression flared in her eyes. She fumbled with the remote and turned the TV off. There hadn't been all that much talking going on in the movie, but the absence of even that much background noise left the motel room way too silent. Duke could practically hear the wheels in her brain turning as she tried to reach a conclusion about his intentions—and her own.

Now what? He heard the question as clearly as if she'd spoken it aloud. He wished the answer were half as clear. He could tumble her onto that bed right this second. The invitation was plain in her eyes.

But he'd had a plan, he reminded himself. A good plan. One that would win her heart, as well as her body. It didn't start with a quick roll in the hay, even if that would put an end once and for all to this awkward indecision that hung over them. She deserved a little wining and dining.

"I'll be dressed in a minute," he said, his gaze still locked with hers.

Before he could change his mind, he went back into the bathroom and slammed the door. Desire made his pulse race and left his fingers unsteady. It took him twice as long as it should have to drag on his clothes, run a comb through his hair and a toothbrush over his teeth.

He even pulled a bottle of that after-shave from his bag, the kind Josh and Zack thought all girls liked, and splashed on a little. He supposed there was something to be said for the spicy scent the boys had chosen for him one Christmas, but as far as he could tell, there was nothing wrong with plain old soap and water.

He gazed at himself in the mirror and shook his head. What was wrong with him? He was acting like a besotted schoolboy. If he wasn't careful someone would get the idea that he was in love. Of course, he knew better. With any luck, Dani wouldn't see through the charade and guess that he thought love was a fool's game.

Before he could have another bout with second thoughts about shortchanging her, he opened the door. "Ready?"

"As ready as I'll ever be," she said, "since I only have the clothes on my back."

"Just be thankful you didn't get drenched the way I did," he said. "Do you want to drive back up to the restaurant or make a dash for it? It's undercover most of the way."

"Dashing will be fine."

She meant it, too. She sprinted ahead of him so fast, he realized that she was every bit as nervous as he was about being alone together in that room.

Though the motel was fully occupied, they were the only two people in the dining room.

"I hurry everyone," Mr. Perez announced with a beaming smile. "I know this is very special occasion. A honeymoon, yes?"

Duke let the guesswork pass. He had a feeling there would be enough discussion about Mr. Perez's conclusions with Dani once they reached their table.

Sure enough, Mr. Perez had no sooner filled their glasses with champagne and vanished into the kitchen than she turned on Duke.

"Honeymoon?" she inquired sweetly. "Where would he get an idea like that?"

"I told him tonight was special, that's all," Duke declared. "He obviously drew his own conclusions."

"Conclusions that merited fresh flowers, candlelight and champagne, I see."

"Actually, those were my ideas."

Her eyes widened. "Really? Fascinating. Is the mariachi band warming up in the back?"

Duke chuckled. "Probably, but if it is you can thank Mr. Perez for it. I was content with the jukebox. It has some really terrific oldies on it."

She stared hard. "You checked out the jukebox, too?"

"Of course. You can't slow dance to just anything on a first date."

"Is that so?"

"Of course not. It has to be romantic, memorable."

"Just one question. When did this go from being a business trip to being a date?" She tilted her head and regarded him thoughtfully. "When you saw the beds, perhaps?"

Duke shook his head and regarded her solemnly. He reached across the table and brushed a tendril of hair away from her cheek, then followed the curve until he cupped her chin. "No. I got this idea the first time I laid eyes on you."

She didn't blink and look away as he'd expected. Instead, she smiled. It was like sunshine breaking through clouds. Duke knew in that instant that he was more than halfway to reaching his goal.

If the rest of the night went even one-quarter as smoothly as this, by morning there was no way she wouldn't say yes when he asked her to marry him. He would find a jewelry store, if he had to bribe the manager to open it on a Sunday morning, and insist on picking out a ring before they ever left Fort Worth. He wanted her well and truly committed to being his before they ever got back to Los Pinos.

"You're looking very smug all of a sudden," she observed.

"Not smug," he insisted. "Pleased. I can't tell you how much I've wanted to share an evening like this with you."

"Stranded in a storm with me smelling like a barn?"

"If you're trying to spoil the mood, forget it. You look beautiful, and you smell like flowers."

"That is flowers you're smelling," she pointed out. "Either that or the after-shave you have on."

"You don't like it? The boys promised me all girls loved it. They picked it out special."

Dani grinned. "The boys have been coaching you?"

"Just on a few of the finer points of courtship."

"Tell them they missed the boat on the after-shave. Soap and water suits me just fine."

"I'll shower again the minute we get back to the room," he offered.

She swallowed hard at the promise. Duke had a hunch she was mentally climbing into that shower with him. Suddenly, she regarded him with suspicion.

"You're playing with my head, aren't you?"

"Am I?"

"You bet."

"How, precisely, am I doing that?"

"You're deliberately planting provocative ideas."

He worked hard to hold back a triumphant grin. "You're having provocative ideas about the two of us?" he inquired innocently. "You can't possibly hold me responsible for what goes on in your head."

"Of course, I can. You're sneaky and devious that way."

"Ever stop to think that maybe you're the one with the wicked mind? You were watching X-rated cable, you know."

"That was an accident," she protested. "Once it was right there in front of my eyes I couldn't seem to look away, sort of like stumbling on a wreck on the highway."

"An interesting comparison."

She scowled at him. "I wasn't comparing sex and traffic accidents."

"Good, because they don't have a lot in common as far as I can see. Sex is a whole lot more fun, to say nothing of way less deadly, at least if it's done right. We could talk about it more, if you like."

"You're doing it again," she accused.

"Doing what?"

"Putting those images into my head."

"Darlin', it seems to me you just have a one-track mind."

She sighed heavily at that. "Maybe I do," she conceded. "But it wasn't true until I met you."

Duke barely contained a victorious shout. "Fascinating," he said quietly.

"To the contrary, it's actually pretty terrifying how badly I want you," she admitted.

She looked so lost and vulnerable that Duke wanted to scoop her up and comfort her…right before he seduced her. He settled for taking her soft hand in his and brushing his lips across her knuckles.

"Don't look so scared, darlin'. We're going to be sensational together."

For how long? He could practically read the unspoken question in her eyes. Because she needed to know this much—and he needed to make it very clear, he answered her unspoken question aloud.

"Stop worrying, darlin'. We're going to be sensational forever."

Chapter Thirteen

The entire evening had been calculated to destroy her unspoken resolve. That much was obvious to Dani as she slipped into Duke's arms for yet another slow dance.

What was less clear was why he had gone to so much trouble. After a couple of glasses of bubbly champagne and a few spins around the deserted dance floor, the answer was fuzzier than ever.

Okay, he wanted to seduce her. Nothing unclear or unexpected about that. But he also seemed determined to make the whole evening memorable.

Not that he had to worry with regard to the sex, she thought wryly. She was already anticipating making love with Duke so eagerly that he couldn't possibly think she needed additional persuading. There wasn't a doubt in her mind that he would make love with the same passion with which he tackled everything in his life.

No, he seemed to be after more than her surrender in bed. Champagne, candles, fresh flowers, they all added up to a man on a romantic mission, a forever kind of mission.

"Stop thinking so hard," he advised, regarding her with amusement.

Her gaze snapped up to clash with his. Was the man psychic or what? "I just wish I could figure out what you're up to," she said a little wistfully.

"Who says I'm up to something?"

"You do. Every now and then this vaguely guilty expression flits across your face. What's that about?"

He shrugged. "I can't imagine. I don't feel the least bit guilty about anything."

"Not even luring me to Fort Worth with a storm on the way?"

He chuckled at the accusation and executed a tricky spin designed to rob her of the ability to speak.

"Are you giving me credit for controlling the weather?" he inquired lightly as she tried to get her equilibrium back.

"No, just taking advantage of it."

"Darlin', a wise man takes advantage of all life's opportunities."

"So whatever plotting has been going on in that head of yours began when the first drop of rain fell earlier this afternoon and not a moment before?" she asked skeptically.

He did look vaguely uncomfortable at that. "Not exactly."

As one song ended and there was a pause before the next, she took the opportunity to look him in the eye. "When exactly did this particular opportunity present itself?" she inquired.

"Does it really matter?"

"It does to me. Let's just call it a test of faith."

"Meaning?"

"Meaning, I want to see if you have enough faith in me to tell me the truth."

He stared hard at her, as if searching for loopholes. Dani kept her gaze unblinking.

"Okay, okay," he finally mumbled. "When the boys started talking about wanting to learn to ride, I saw an opportunity to get you alone for a while. Just for the day, though."

"Not overnight?"

As the music began again, he grinned unrepentantly and swept her back into his arms. "No," he insisted, "this is just a bonus."

Dani couldn't help it. She chuckled. "There now, that wasn't so difficult, was it? See how honesty pays?"

"I suppose that depends on whether you ask the Perezes to let you bunk with them or come back to our room with me." His gaze locked with hers. "So, Dani, it's the moment of truth. What's it going to be?"

She should have left him dangling, held off on an answer until dessert just to torment him, but she couldn't do it. "I suppose, since you've gone to so much trouble..."

His lips began a slow curve into a smile. "The room?"

"The room," she agreed softly.

"Now?" he inquired with ego-boosting eagerness, already heading back to their table for the check.

She grinned and shook her head, then deliberately pulled out her chair and sat. "Settle down, cowboy," she advised. "This is one opportunity that doesn't need to be claimed in a rush."

For a while there Duke's heart had been in his throat. Dani had seen straight through him, guessed all—well, almost all—of his devious little secrets and, he'd been almost certain, had been about to bring his whole scheme crashing down around his head. That she hadn't was testament to the depth of her feelings. He wondered if she even recognized how revealing her reactions had been. He doubted it. She would hate that he could see into her heart, especially since she'd worked so hard to hide all the soft spots.

Comforting himself that his goal was all but certain, Duke settled back in his chair and forced himself to relax. It wasn't all that difficult. He simply set out to enjoy the play of candlelight across her face, the shimmering of gold it set off in her hair. He relished the hitching of her breath whenever his fingers chanced to graze hers.

In fact, he discovered that the slow build of anticipation had its own reward. It had been a long time since he'd felt the kind of insistent, gut-deep hunger for a woman that he was feeling for Dani by the time they clasped hands and walked slowly back to their room.

The temperature hadn't dropped nearly as precipitously as had been predicted. The rain had softened to little more than a gentle shower, leaving the air cleansed and crisp.

To his amazement, Dani stepped out from under the shelter of the covered walkway and tilted her face up to the sky. A fine mist settled on her skin, leaving it as dewy as a spring morning and a hundred times more appealing. She held out her arms as if to embrace the night. The gesture was so totally unselfconscious, so gloriously uninhibited and happy that Duke found himself joining her, getting soaked for the second time that night. He hardly even noticed.

"Isn't it wonderful?" she murmured, meeting his gaze.

"It's wet," he observed, concluding that she was definitely a little tipsy.

"It reminds me of 'Singing in the Rain,' one of my all-time favorite movies," she said, looking nostalgic.

He recalled the specific scene vividly. "Gene Kelly dancing in the street," he said with a smile. "Are you planning to launch into song or dance any second now?"

"No," she said with a wistful sigh. "I can't sing and I can't dance."

"Who says?" he protested. "No one's grading you out here. Come on, darlin'. Go for it."

He encouraged her by whistling the first few bars of the song. She did a little skip, then something vaguely resembling a tap routine. She was no Gene Kelly, that was for sure, but her face was glowing and her eyes were sparkling under the twinkling display of neon that splashed color across the damp pavement.

"You, too," she insisted, grabbing his hand.

"I'll sing," he offered instead, belting out what he considered to be a credible rendition of the movie's title song. He grabbed her off her feet and twirled her around for the sheer exhilarating fun of it. It was, if he did say so himself, quite a finale.

Or, perhaps, an extraordinary opening, if the main production was yet to come. Either way, he was well and truly caught up in the storyline.

Especially when her body slid slowly down his as he lowered her feet back to the ground. Eyes wide, she met his gaze evenly, then slowly, so slowly that his body throbbed with the anticipation of it, she lifted her hands to his cheeks and framed his face. When she stood on tiptoe and kissed him, he was more or less convinced that the whole state of Texas shook.

"Oh, baby," he whispered raggedly, when he could catch his breath at all. "That was a real show-stopper."

She grinned at him, her expression very feminine and very smug. "Come along. I'm not waiting around out here for the applause. Something tells me it'll be a long time coming, and I have better things to do."

"Really? You turning brazen on me, darlin'?" he inquired hopefully.

"I'm thinking about it," she said, leading the way to the doorstep of their room.

Duke decided he was enjoying her seduction far too much to race right inside. Instead of opening the door, he leaned down and stole one more kiss, a real barn burner of a kiss.

It was Dani who eventually dragged her mouth away from his and stared up at him with dazed eyes. "Inside," she murmured. It came out as part command, part plea.

Duke nodded. "Fine by me."

"Open the door, then."

"I think I'll leave that up to you."

Her gaze faltered. "But you have the key." Alarm flared for a second in her eyes. "You do have the key, don't you?"

"Sure do. It's in my pocket. Anytime you want to slide your hand in there and get it," he suggested provocatively, "we can go right on in."

She regarded him with amusement. "Think you're real smart, don't you?"

He feigned a disinterested expression. "Smart enough."

"Okay, mister, let's see if you can take what you dish out," she said, offering her own challenge.

The glittering dare in her eyes made Duke vaguely uneasy. He braced himself for the torment of her touch. It would be interesting to see just how far she would go to prove which of them was the more clever.

"Which pocket?" she inquired with mild curiosity, after a visual survey of the alternatives.

When he would have replied, she touched a silencing finger to his lips. "Never mind. I think I'll just take my time and figure it out."

She stepped in very close, until her breasts were pressed against his chest and her warm breath was fanning across his cheek. Her arms circled his waist and she very, very slowly ran one hand up the curve of his backside until she reached the top of his pocket. Duke's blood began to hammer in his veins.

She searched that pocket so thoroughly and with such lingering, devilish caresses he thought for sure his heart would burst.

Then, when he was sure that his jeans couldn't possibly be any more uncomfortable, she did the exact same thing all over again with the other back pocket.

"Not here," she finally concluded, regarding him gravely. "Now where could that key be?"

Duke was totally incapable of replying. Maybe if he could have, maybe if he'd snatched the darn thing out himself, he could have saved himself from the wicked probing of his remaining pockets.

She slid her hands up his chest, examined the pockets in his shirt with care, finally satisfying herself that the key was elsewhere. He was breathing hard when she was done.

Then she moved on to the front pockets of his jeans. Deft fingers managed to skim far more than the depths of those pockets. With some sort of uncanny intuition she had managed to save the one that actually held the key until last. By then he was relatively certain that his body was one caress away from coming apart.

As she slowly and triumphantly removed the key,

he stepped back so fast he almost tumbled off the curb. "Satisfied?" he muttered.

"Not yet," she said, giving him a saucy smile. "You?"

"Definitely not yet."

"Well, then, I guess we should go inside before we make a spectacle of ourselves."

Duke regarded her curiously. "What just happened here?"

"I'm pretty sure I proved that I know how to get you all hot and bothered," she said with obvious satisfaction. She opened the door and stepped inside, then gave him a head-to-toe survey that could have melted steel before adding, "It remains to be seen if you can do the same."

He shook his head. "Darlin', don't you know how dangerous it is to issue that kind of a challenge to a man as close to the end of his rope as I am?"

"No," she said, then added innocently, "Perhaps you should show me."

Duke stepped inside and slammed the door so hard behind him, it rocked on its hinges. Dani grinned at the impatient gesture.

"Careful there. If we want any privacy, we need that door right where it is."

"Very amusing," he said and reached for her.

She put up very little resistance when he tugged her into his arms and settled his mouth over hers. There was nothing careful or tentative about this claiming. He was a man possessed. He wanted to taste her, to make very sure she knew that from this night on she belonged only to him.

Duke had never felt this demanding need for a woman. Not that he hadn't enjoyed sex. He had the usual appetite for the feel of a soft body beneath his own, for being surrounded by slick, moist heat.

But this hot, urgent passion seemed to run deeper than that. It was as if he needed to prove that beyond the teasing and the provocation, beyond the flirting and kisses, there was more. For the first time in his life, he felt as if he were putting some new part of himself on the line.

Perhaps his heart.

His pulse hitched at the thought. But not even the terror that should have followed would have been enough to get him to walk out of this room tonight.

Oddly enough, though, the panic never came. He would have to figure out why later.

In fact at the moment, as his fingers made short work of buttons and snaps, then skimmed over bare flesh, all he felt was the exhilaration of a man who was right where he wanted to be, with the woman with whom he belonged.

Forcing himself to drag in a deep, calming breath, he slowed down. He lifted Dani off her feet, then placed her on the bed as reverently as he'd ever touched anything in his life.

Dani returned his gaze with a hooded, smoldering look of her own. He was relieved by that, glad that there was no evidence of the lost, vulnerable woman he had met a few months ago. Whatever she felt for him in her heart, she was meeting him tonight as a strong, decisive woman, the kind of woman he'd seen evidenced in her work. Maybe, he thought, he'd played some small part in giving her back her confidence.

His gaze danced over her, then took a slower, lingering survey. She was so lovely. Small and delicate in many ways, there was a surprising, but unmistakable strength about her. He followed the subtle definition in her arms, stopped to savor the gentle sweep of a shoulder, then moved on to admire the generous curve of her breasts. He trailed a finger down that soft slope to a tip that was as hard as a pebble beneath his touch, then repeated the action on her other breast until she gasped with pleasure and her eyes drifted closed.

When his mouth closed over one sensitive peak, her eyes flew open and her hands tunneled through his hair as if to keep him there.

Duke was far from finished, though. Each breast was but a stopping point on his journey of discovery. He wanted to know every inch of her, to discover textures and tastes and secret pleasure spots. He wanted her to remember every second, every caress.

"Duke?"

He stopped his intimate examination of a sensitive spot on the inside of her thigh and met her gaze. "Yes?"

"Look at me," she pleaded softly. "Look at me and make love to me. I want you inside me now."

"In a minute, darlin'. I'm not quite through with my survey."

"Your survey is making me crazy," she confessed.

He hid a grin. "That's the general idea."

"But I want to make you crazy, too."

"Oh, baby, you do," he vowed. He reached for her hand. "Here, feel." When he placed her hand over the hard shaft of his arousal, a slow smile spread across her face. Confidence returned. Her gaze met his boldly.

"If that's the case," she said, "then let's go for it."

"We're not racing a clock, are we?"

"I just thought it would be good to seize the opportunity," she pointed out.

Duke chuckled. "Like you told me, this opportunity isn't going anywhere. In fact, we're just now starting to take full advantage of it."

He set out to prove to her the exquisite torture of slow, deliberate caresses and deep, bone-melting kisses. She was slick with perspiration and writhing against the sheets by the time he knelt between her thighs and slowly entered her.

The moist, welcoming heat claimed him as surely as he'd set out to claim her. She was slick and tight and eager. The movement of her hips was timed perfectly to him as if they'd learned this rhythm in another lifetime and only in each other's arms. He was all but certain it had never been like this before.

Duke was struck by the stunning thought that this was what people meant when they referred to soul mates. That had always been an elusive concept to him, the idea that destiny chose two people and saw to it that they came together for eternity.

But as their bodies melded, as wave after wave of stunning pleasure washed over them, he began to wonder if he hadn't been a little too quick to dismiss the notion.

When Dani's cry of release shimmered around him, it was all he could do to hold back a triumphant shout. She was his now, as surely as if she'd already said yes to the proposal he had yet to make.

As for him, if he looked very, very closely inside his heart, he had a feeling he might discover that he was just as much her captive. To his astonishment, rather than being panicked by that, all he felt was a sort of intense, heady relief.

Dani stretched languorously. She had never felt better in her life. As long as she didn't allow a lot of doubts to start crowding in, she would be just fine. Better than fine. She would be magnificent.

There was one sure way to see that doubts remained at bay. She slid across the mattress and tucked herself up against Duke, pausing to admire the hard planes and angles of his body. There wasn't an ounce of spare flesh on him. And the man generated enough body heat to warm all of Texas. Her inquisitive, probing hands slid across his belly, then down. He moaned softly, then came wide-awake with a start. After a moment of obvious disorientation, he regarded her with amusement.

"What are you up to?" he inquired.

"Isn't that obvious?"

"Explain it to me, anyway."

She grinned. "Just checking to see if this was one of those rare times when opportunity knocked twice."

He regarded her balefully. "Twice? I'm fairly certain I recall it knocking several times during the night.''

"That was then. This is now.''

He studied her face intently. ''Trying to keep the regrets at bay, by any chance?''

Dani stared at him in shock. Was she so obvious? "Why would you ask that?"·

"Because I know you better than you think I do.'' He grinned that lazy, sexy grin that destroyed her defenses. "Come on now, no regrets.''

"Easy for you to say. This doesn't solve anything between us, Duke, not really.''

"I'm perfectly willing to make it legal,'' he said. "Just say the word.''

She stared at him. His expression was neutral. Clearly he didn't intend to give away whether he was serious or not. "You want to marry me?'' she asked, spelling it out so there could be no mistake.

"You didn't think this was some casual, one-night stand for me, did you? I'm not that kind of man.'' He shook his head with exaggerated sorrow. "Never mind. I'll prove it to you.''

"There's no need.''

"Of course, there is. You can't marry me, if you don't trust me.''

Warning signals that had apparently been on the blink for too many hours were recharged now. They were clanging like the very dickens. "I'm not going to marry you, period,'' she insisted, even though the pull of the idea made her limp with longing.

"We'll see,'' he said smugly.

Dani sighed. "Duke, we're consenting adults here. This doesn't require a proposal to make it okay."

"Never said it did." He shot her a chin-up, defiant look. "I'm asking you to marry me just the same."

"No," she said again, though her stomach was as jittery as if she'd said yes.

"Why not?" He met her gaze evenly. "And don't try telling me you don't love me, because I'm not buying it."

"Well, aren't you the cocky one?" she retorted. "Just because we made love doesn't mean I'm *in love*."

"Nope," he agreed solemnly. "That's not proof all by itself."

"Then would you mind telling me where you got such a cockamamie idea?" Maybe then she could see to it that she never, ever did anything similar again.

"You women have your intuition," he said. "We men have other ways."

"Such as?"

"Darlin', I'd be going against the code if I gave it away."

"Code? What code? Gave what away?" she asked, thoroughly exasperated.

"It's a guy thing."

She stared at him incredulously. "It's a guy thing? Well, this is a girl thing." She climbed out of bed and draped herself in the bedspread, figuring that delivering her tirade stark naked would take a little of the sass out of it. "I am not now nor do I ever intend to be in love with you. I will not marry you."

Duke didn't seem to be the least bit distressed. "We'll see."

Dani marched off to the bathroom and slammed the door behind her. When it was closed, she leaned heavily against it.

"Well, damn," she murmured.

How was she supposed to fight a man who was offering her the very thing she wanted most in the world: Marriage and a family every bit as strong as the one into which she'd been welcomed as a child.

By telling herself a thousand times a day that he didn't really love her, she reminded herself. The only hitch to that was the fact that last night, in his arms, it had felt an awful lot like he might be loving her back.

Chapter Fourteen

Duke recognized an ambush when he saw one. Jordan had asked him to drop by Dolan's and pick up a package for him while he was out to lunch. It should have occurred to him that Sharon Lynn would have been more than happy to have the blasted package delivered.

So, because he wasn't thinking straight, hadn't been thinking straight ever since he'd returned from Fort Worth, he walked into the drugstore as innocent as a lamb. There, clearly just waiting for him, were both Sharon Lynn and Jenny. They perked up visibly at the sight of him.

Duke sighed. Everyone had maintained a polite, if clearly expectant facade right through Christmas and New Year's. Now, since no ring or engagement announcement had been forthcoming, apparently Sharon

Lynn and Jenny had been designated by the family to get to the bottom of what had gone on between him and Dani on their trip and what was likely to go on between them from now through eternity.

"Afternoon, ladies," he said, figuring he could bluff his way through the conversation or else run like hell. Since the latter wasn't a real option, he decided he'd better brazen it out.

"Hey, Duke, come on and join me," Jenny suggested, patting the stool beside her.

"I really need to get back to the office," he said, flashing her a smile. "Jordan just asked me to pick something up for him while I was out grabbing lunch."

She regarded him skeptically. "Have you actually had lunch yet?" she asked with typical Adams directness.

He sighed. "No."

Sharon Lynn beamed at him. "Well, then, no more excuses. Uncle Jordan can wait a few more minutes. Sit right down. What'll it be? A hamburger? Grilled cheese? BLT?"

Duke wondered which one would be the quickest to prepare and gulp down. "Grilled cheese," he said.

"Fries with that?"

Fries would take too long, especially in the quantity Sharon Lynn served them up. They would have to be eaten one by one. "No, not today."

"And to drink? Coffee?"

No way. He would have to wait for coffee to cool. "Just water," he said.

Apparently, his nervousness was transparent. The

two women exchanged an amused glance. He, in turn, regarded them suspiciously.

"Okay, what are you two up to?" he asked.

"Nothing," Sharon Lynn claimed.

"Absolutely nothing," Jenny concurred.

He scowled in Sharon Lynn's direction. "When are you and Kyle Mason setting a date?" he inquired, hoping to divert her attention from his love life by focusing on hers.

She grinned. "The date's set. First Saturday in June. He finally got around to proposing in the middle of college football on New Year's Day. The man's timing is impeccable. Now there's no way I can doubt how much he loves me. He actually stopped watching the Aggies for a full fifteen minutes." She grinned and waved her ring under his nose. "I hope you'll be there."

"Of course." So much for that tactic, he thought, turning to Jenny. Before he could ask, she held up her hand to stop any inquiry he was planning.

"No love life. Not interested. No time," she declared.

He grinned at her vehemence. "And how does Harlan feel about that?"

Sharon Lynn chuckled as Jenny heaved a heavy sigh. "Grandpa isn't too thrilled with her attitude," Sharon Lynn confided. "In fact, I'd say she is on his personal to-do list. Get Jenny a husband, right up there in big, bold print."

"Oh, go suck an egg," Jenny retorted.

Duke regarded her with amusement. "Let that be

a lesson to you. If you don't want anyone meddling in your love life, stay out of theirs.''

Jenny's gaze narrowed. "Meaning?"

"Meaning I could very easily join forces with your father," Duke warned.

Both women hooted at that, which wasn't quite the reaction he'd been hoping for.

"You poor man," Jenny said. "Don't you realize that you and Dani are way, way above me on his list? In fact, I'd say at the moment you two are his number one priority. He's always preferred to hedge his bets and go with a sure thing. I'm way too speculative at the moment."

Duke sat, silently absorbing the news. He waited for the panic to set in, just as he had over and over again in that motel in Fort Worth. It didn't come. In fact, in a curious way, he was relieved that he had allies, powerful allies. He'd felt surprisingly disappointed and disgruntled when Dani had flat-out turned him down in Forth Worth.

Why was that? he wondered, trying to think back over the past few months. He was a bright man. Surely, he could analyze this thing with Dani from start to finish and reach a logical conclusion.

It had started as a game. Duke was willing to admit that much, even though it didn't say much for him. Then it had moved on to a game he was playing for his sons' benefit.

Now, much to his amazement, he realized that the stakes were totally personal and very, very important. He'd gone and fallen in love with the woman. He tried to imagine his life without her, and he couldn't.

All he saw was a bleak and empty future, the exact kind of future he'd once considered his due for all his sins.

Lately, though, he'd had a taste of brighter possibilities and he knew he would never be happy unless he did everything in his power to make them happen. He wanted more than a mother for the kids. To his astonishment, he'd discovered that what he wanted most of all was a wife. He wanted a woman who could make his heart leap simply by walking into a room. He wanted a woman who listened and teased and taunted. He wanted a companion, a friend and a lover.

He wanted Dani.

Of course, realizing what was in his heart was a snap compared to convincing Dani what was in hers. He looked from Sharon Lynn to Jenny. Both women were studying him with blatant curiosity.

"I'm not your problem, ladies," he declared, summing up in a nutshell the conclusion he'd just reached.

"Explain," Sharon Lynn said, her elbows on the counter and her chin cupped in her hands as she regarded him intently.

"It's Dani," Jenny concluded without waiting for his reply. "She's holding out."

"Seems to be," he agreed.

"Why?" Sharon Lynn asked. "Have you told her how you feel?"

"I asked her to marry me."

Jenny didn't seem the least bit surprised by that. She waved her hand impatiently. "That isn't what

Sharon Lynn asked. Have you told her how you feel?''

Duke hesitated to admit that he was just coming to grips himself with the fact that he was in love with her. In the natural, old-fashioned order of things, he supposed he should have reached that conclusion before he hauled her into bed. He definitely should have reached it before proposing.

"Sleeping with her isn't an answer," Jenny said, stunning him into silence. "Proposing marriage is nice, but that's not enough, either."

"In other words, have you mentioned that you love her?" Sharon Lynn prodded more specifically.

Duke cleared his throat.

Jenny sighed. "No. The answer's no, isn't it?" She glanced at Sharon Lynn. "Men are such idiots. Now do you see why I'm content to live my nice, peaceful existence without one?"

Sharon Lynn rolled her eyes. "Women like you always fall the hardest," she warned. "I can hardly wait."

"Oh, shut up. We're not talking about me," Jenny said, turning away from Sharon Lynn and facing Duke squarely. "Now what do you intend to do to get this marriage business with Dani straightened out before she does something crazy like going back with that awful Rob Hilliard?"

"Hilliard?" Duke demanded tightly. "What the hell does he have to do with anything?"

"He's been calling again," Sharon Lynn said. "He brought the girls by over the holidays. Dani cried for an hour after they left."

That was all news to Duke. Bad news. He had warned the guy to stay away. The only way to ensure that happening, though, was to get Dani to marry him. Unfortunately, though, he was fresh out of ideas. Aside from acknowledging that what he was feeling these days was love, he was forced to admit that he was stymied. Finding oil where it shouldn't be was a breeze compared to this.

"I was hoping you two could make a suggestion," he said, throwing himself on their mercy. Something told him he could trust them. They both had Dani's best interests at heart. "You seem to have all the answers."

"Now you're talking," Jenny said approvingly.

"Something dramatic," Sharon Lynn said.

"Something simple," Jenny countered. "Dani would be embarrassed by dramatic."

Duke thought of Dani's performance in the motel parking lot, not her singing and dancing, but that sexy slip-sliding game she had played for the room key. She was not half as demure as Jenny apparently thought she was. He thought maybe dramatic would be for the best. Kelly had shared some of the more outrageous things Jordan had done to win her heart. Perhaps he should try a few of those on her daughter. Maybe Dani would be charmed by the nostalgia of it, if nothing else.

"Thanks for the help, ladies," he said, climbing off the stool. "I think I'll take it from here."

"But we haven't come up with a really good plan," Jenny protested.

"And you never even got your sandwich," Sharon Lynn said.

"That's okay. You've provided plenty of inspiration," he assured them, grinning at the self-satisfied smirks they exchanged.

"Keep us posted on your progress," Sharon Lynn pleaded.

"Sweetheart, if there's any progress, I'm sure you won't need me to drop by and fill you in. With an Adams involved, word will spread like wildfire."

Ever since her return from Fort Worth, Dani had been dragging around, her mood despondent. She'd been snapping at Maggie at the clinic until the poor girl had threatened to quit unless her boss's mood improved.

"You need a man in your life," Maggie said. "In my opinion, you're frustrated."

Little did she know, Dani thought sourly. She'd never been less frustrated in her life, sexually speaking. Emotionally, however, was another thing entirely. Rob's impromptu little visit with the girls hadn't helped, either. They'd all been in tears by the time he packed them up again and took off, her refusal to reconsider their relationship ringing in his ears.

Apparently, word of her crummy attitude was spreading, too. Everyone in the family was watching her as if they expected her to break out with chicken pox or maybe hives at any second. They were hovering, their expressions alternately sympathetic and hopeful. Well, the whole blasted lot of them could go jump in the creek, she thought miserably. Their lives weren't on the line. Hers was.

Duke's proposal echoed in her head at the most inopportune moments. Memories of the way his hands had molded and shaped her body with intimate precision, drawing ragged sighs and heartfelt gasps, left her feeling so hot and bothered she was tempted to turn the air conditioning on, even though it was barely freezing outside.

It would be so easy to say yes, so uncomplicated to cave in to Duke's pressure. If, of course, he'd pressured her. Instead, the man was nowhere to be found. She'd even dropped in on her father at work, hoping to catch a glimpse of Duke. Of course, it had been lunchtime, she consoled herself. He'd probably just slipped out for a sandwich.

She declined Jordan's offer to take her out somewhere and wandered down to Dolan's herself. Sharon Lynn and Jenny had been huddled together at the counter, their expressions guilty as sin when they spotted her.

"You just missed Duke," Sharon Lynn said a little too brightly.

"Was he here for lunch?"

The question drew another guilty look. Sharon Lynn shrugged. "Not really. He was running an errand for Uncle Jordan."

"I see," Dani said and slipped onto a stool. "Can I have a hot fudge sundae, please?"

"Now?" Sharon Lynn said as if it were the most scandalous request she'd ever heard. "In the middle of the day?"

Dani scowled at her. "Do you have a problem with that?"

"No, of course not," her cousin declared and rushed to scoop up the ice cream. She added extra hot fudge and enough whipped cream to clog the arteries of half the population of Los Pinos.

She and Jenny watched uneasily as Dani silently ate every single bite.

"Man trouble?" Jenny inquired eventually.

"Who, me?"

"Yes, you," Jenny said impatiently. "What's with you and Duke?"

"Nothing," Dani said, noting the amused look the two exchanged. "Okay, what's up? Do you know something I don't?"

"Not a thing," Jenny responded.

"Absolutely nothing," Sharon Lynn concurred.

Dani didn't believe either one of them. There was some sort of scheme afoot. "I hope you're not interfering in this," she said, regarding first one, then the other intently.

"Absolutely not," they assured her dutifully.

"Because if I find out that you have been, I will..." She couldn't think offhand of anything quite dire enough.

"What?" Sharon Lynn prodded, an impudent, teasing glint in her eyes.

"Yes, what will you do?" Jenny inquired, clearly fascinated by the threat.

"I will deliver entire litters of kittens to your doorsteps in the middle of the night," she warned.

"You do that anyway," Jenny said. "White Pines is crawling with them."

"So's our place," Sharon Lynn agreed. "Dad's still trying to figure out how you manage it."

Dani sighed at the failed threat. "Okay, forget the kittens, but I will make you pay. Remember that. And I will do it when you least expect it."

She slid off the stool and headed for the door. She was pretty sure she heard them chuckling when they thought she was too far away to catch them at it. There really were times when having a family that knew you so well could be a nuisance, she thought as she barely resisted the urge to slam the drugstore door behind her.

Since the clinic was already closed for the afternoon, she decided to take a drive out to White Pines. Not that she couldn't expect more of the same taunting from Grandpa Harlan, but at least he usually managed to impart some wisdom along with his teasing.

She found her grandfather in the paddock along with Cody and one of the hands. They were going over a horse that appeared to be lame. She would have offered to check him out herself, but Cody knew every bit as much as she did about this kind of thing. She had some expertise, of course, but small pets were her forte. She was called in to treat large animals only when the vet in the next town couldn't be reached.

Waving to the men, she went into the stables and saddled up the pinto, which had turned out to be a surprisingly quick learner once it concluded that no one here was likely to harm it. He'd put on weight and no longer had that wild look in his eyes.

"You're my pal now, aren't you?" she whispered as he nuzzled her pocket for one of the sugar cubes she invariably kept there for him. She took out two. "Here you go."

Maybe a good, long ride was what she needed. It would clear her head.

The bottom line, she concluded as she raced straight into the wind, was that she wanted desperately to trust her heart. She wanted to admit that she had fallen in love with Duke, but how could she? She kept coming back to the boys.

She knew from her own experience with Jordan that being a stepkid could be just fine, better than fine. But Jordan and her mom had been committed to each other for years, even though it had taken him a long time to recognize what was in his heart.

She and Duke didn't have that same long history. There was every chance that they would fail at making a relationship work. She had thrown herself heart and soul into her relationship with Rob and look at what a mess she'd made of that. They'd even had a four-year foundation to build on. By comparison, this thing with Duke had been a whirlwind courtship.

She was so lost in thought that her grandfather had ridden up beside her before she was even aware he was in the vicinity. He dismounted and walked over to sit beside her on the fence rail.

As his warm gaze settled on her, she saw the worry lines that were clearly etched in his forehead. "You okay, kiddo?"

"More or less."

"Problems with Duke?"

"Nothing but problems," she conceded. "Ever since we came back from Fort Worth, he's been avoiding me. Other than a glimpse or two in a crowd here over the holidays, I never even saw him."

"Maybe he's just giving you time to think."

"I suppose."

He cupped a hand under her chin and forced her to look at him. "So, when are you going to put that boy out of his misery?" he demanded. "He's going around looking like a lovesick puppy and you don't look one bit better. It's time to fish or cut bait, darlin' girl."

"Oh, please," she muttered. "Duke Jenkins couldn't look pitiful if he took acting classes for a lifetime."

"It's true. Jordan says he can't keep his mind on work, either. That's a sure sign a man's in love."

"You know what happened with Rob," she reminded him. "The girls still haven't gotten over it. How can I take that chance again? It wouldn't be fair to Joshua and Zachary, especially since Duke can't even bring himself to admit he has any feelings for me at all."

"Have you admitted you're in love with him?"

The question made her pause. "No," she conceded eventually.

"The way I hear it, he has asked you to marry him. Is that true?"

"Yes, but—"